"Here's your bottle, little Bella."

Jase angled the bottle and she took it, making sweet little baby noises.

Soon Erin leaned in and looked at the bottle. "It's time to burp her."

Okay, he'd heard of burping a baby before…

"Take the bottle out of her mouth, hold her on your shoulder and gently rub her back." He didn't have to look at Erin to know she was grinning. He could hear it in her voice. "That's all there is to it."

Right. He could do this. He just needed to focus—

He must have had a panicked expression, because Miss Fannie broke out in a giggle. "Relax, Jase. You'll be fine."

"Sure, as long as I don't drop the baby. Or drown her in milk. Or forget to burp her—" He shot his gaze toward Erin. "What if I forget to burp her?"

"She'll remind you. She'll cry."

Great. He forgets one little thing and it'll make Bella cry? He'd been right. He was not the man for this job. This was going to be a disaster.

Christina Miller left her nursing job to become a writer and editor so she could read for a living. With two theology degrees, she is a pastor's wife and worship leader. She enjoys exploring museums and hosting Dinner Church in her home. She lives on her family farm with her husband of thirty-two years and Sugar, their talking dog. Contact Christina through Love Inspired, Facebook.com/christinalinstrotmiller or @clmillerbooks.

Books by Christina Miller

Love Inspired

Finding His Family
An Orphan's Hope

Love Inspired Historical

Counterfeit Courtship
An Inconvenient Marriage

Visit the Author Profile page at LoveInspired.com.

An Orphan's Hope

Christina Miller

LOVE INSPIRED
INSPIRATIONAL ROMANCE

LOVE INSPIRED®

INSPIRATIONAL ROMANCE

Recycling programs for this product may not exist in your area.

ISBN-13: 978-1-335-56752-9

An Orphan's Hope

This edition published by arrangement with Harlequin Books S.A.

For questions and comments about the quality of this book, please contact us at CustomerService@Harlequin.com.

Love Inspired
22 Adelaide St. West, 41st Floor
Toronto, Ontario M5H 4E3, Canada
www.LoveInspired.com

Printed in U.S.A.

All things are possible to him that believeth.
—*Mark* 9:23

To our youth pastors, volunteer youth workers and spouses. You do the hardest work of the ministry. I appreciate you.

With special thanks to Judge E. Vincent Davis for your invaluable help.

Chapter One

The only way Jase could get a woman to the altar was by marrying her to another man.

He stood before the wedding guests assembled on the little open-air chapel's lawn. The three-sided structure served as an elegant backdrop, with its Doric columns and marble urns, as the cool afternoon breeze fanned the pages of Jase's open Bible. He'd slipped a crisp white handkerchief into his inner pocket as always, just in case.

As the string quartet played the bridal chorus, the dark-haired bride made her way, alone, up the pathway to her groom. When she took her place before him, Jase corrected himself. No, he hadn't failed to get a bride to this altar. Truth was, in the past three years, two women had met him at this very spot.

And had run away before Jase Armstrong could say "I do."

"Dearly beloved, we are gathered here today in the sight of God..." Reciting by memory the ceremony's opening lines, Jase took in the sights. The stocky groom wiped his palms on his gray suit pants. The cute blond bridesmaid, with her matching pink flowers and dress, kept her laser-sharp focus on her friend in white. The bride's distracted gaze flitted from the chapel flowers to the nearby gazebo to the ancient mansion beyond.

Everywhere except her groom.

On the alert now, Jase raised his voice. "Not to be entered into lightly..."

At his words, the bride's face paled, her pink bouquet trembling in her hand. She shook her head almost imperceptibly.

No...

Jase had seen that look before. Twice.

He turned slightly, toward the bridesmaid, and caught her eye. With raised brows, he tilted his head in the bride's direction, silently asking if her friend was all right.

A small line appeared between the bridesmaid's brows as she took a step forward.

"If any person here can show cause why these two people should not be joined in holy matrimony," Jase said, having no choice but to go on, "speak now or forever hold your peace."

The bride's free hand crept upward to her mouth. She shook her head again. "I—I can't," she whispered, her gaze now shifted to the brick-lined gravel path. "I'm sorry, Robert. I just can't."

She dropped her bouquet on the grass, then kicked off her high-heeled white shoes and ran toward the gazebo, her veil billowing behind her and her lacy train trailing along the ground.

Jase reached inside his suit coat, grabbed his handkerchief and thrust it toward the bridesmaid. "Go after her."

The bridesmaid hesitated only a moment, her big brown eyes wide, before she snatched the handkerchief and raced toward the bride. Except this girl ran in her fancy shoes. "Danielle, wait!"

Jase drew a deep breath to call out to her, too, then closed his mouth and turned to the groom instead. What could Jase say to the bride that would help the situation, considering he hadn't been able to stop either of his former fiancées from leaving him at the altar? No, his place was with the groom.

Not that he knew what to say to him, either...

Lord, help me now, because I've got nothing that will help this guy. He could have said the

Lord was faithful. Time would ease the pain a little. God could give a jilted groom meaningful work that would take his mind off the fact that no woman would ever love him for who he was. Trouble was, that wouldn't help Robert any more than it would have helped Jase if anyone had told him these truths.

But he could never tell the groom the lie that well-meaning friends and family had told Jase: *You'll find another woman. One who will value your ministry and even help you in your calling.*

"I— What just happened?" The groom looked as pale as the bride had before she'd sprinted across the lawn like one of the track stars in Jase's church youth group. He scrubbed his round face with both hands. "What's she doing?"

Jase squeezed the man's shoulder, all the memories and gut-knifing pain roaring over him again like a hurricane tide. "I'm sorry…"

"I'm going after her." Robert's countenance changed, his jaw tight and his eyes wet with unshed tears. He took off toward his would-be bride. "Danielle—Dannie, sweetheart—" Robert called, his voice cracking.

Trust me, it's useless, man. But go ahead and try.

Jase turned his attention toward the wide-eyed, murmuring audience of twenty or so friends and family, most of whom stood now and gazed in obvious horror toward the drama. Danielle sat in the gazebo with the bridesmaid as Robert ran toward them.

"Everybody, this is a distressing turn of events," Jase said, raising his voice, "but please be seated and give the couple as much privacy as we can. As soon as we know their wishes, we'll go from there."

Before he could figure out what to say next, amid the quiet rustling of wedding guests sitting down again, a soft cry sounded from behind him.

He spun toward the stone bench beside the chapel—the one his octogenarian boss, Miss Fannie Swan, occupied every time a couple rented her wedding venue. Now the sweet lady stood next to the bench, swaying as if she was about to faint.

"Miss Fannie!" Jase raced to her side, but before he could reach her, she dropped to the ground. He knelt beside her in the grass. Shook her shoulder a little.

No response.

"Somebody call nine-one-one," he said, and then he realized he'd yelled it at the top of his lungs.

He felt for a carotid pulse. Was it too slow?

He wasn't sure. Her breath came in tiny puffs, and that scared him a little.

Jase tried to recall everything he'd learned in his college first-aid course, but all he could remember was to elevate the feet. He glanced around for something to prop them on. The chair seats were too high for her petite stature. Pillows would work, but they'd have to go all the way to the house to get them.

He picked up her hand and tapped it with the tips of his fingers. "Miss Fannie." He raised his voice. "Miss Fannie. Can you hear me?"

"I have nine-one-one on speakerphone," one of the guests said. He laid the phone on the ground next to Jase.

"What's your emergency?" the female voice said on the other end of the line.

"It's Miss Fannie Swan," Jase said, recognizing the dispatcher's voice. The grandma of one of his youth group girls. "She fainted or something, Miss Marsha. This is Jase Armstrong."

"Is she breathing, Jase?"

He checked to make sure she still was and caught sight of the bridesmaid dashing their way. She hit the ground on her knees, all but skidding the last twelve inches. "She's breathing, but it doesn't look right," he said.

"Fast and shallow," the bridesmaid said,

pressing her fingers to Miss Fannie's neck. "Pulse slow and a little thready."

Jase stood and moved back. The bridesmaid clearly knew more about this than he did. He picked up the phone and held it close to her.

She raised one of Miss Fannie's eyelids, then the other. "Pupils are normal." Then she gently pinched the skin on the older lady's forearm, just above the wrist. "Tissue turgor is poor. Lips are dry. She looks dehydrated."

"Jase, I'm sending the ambulance," Marsha said. "Are you at Rosewood?"

"Yeah, we were in the middle of a wedding." Kind of.

Miss Fannie opened her eyes as Jase relayed her medical information to Marsha. "What happened?"

She raised her head and shoulders as if wanting to get up, but the bridesmaid gave her a sweet smile and gently guided her back to the ground. "You fainted, ma'am. Do you have any pain?"

Miss Fannie shook her head.

"Then just lie there and rest a little and let me take care of you. Reverend, if you don't mind getting your suit pants dirty, please sit here, cross-legged, at her feet."

He frowned a little, settling himself on the

ground as she'd asked. He couldn't care less about his pants, but why—

She slipped off Miss Fannie's rhinestone-studded silver shoes and laid her feet on Jase's knees. "Adjust your posture to keep her feet as high as is comfortable for you."

Oh.

After he'd followed her instructions, Jase realized his friend was lying on the ground in full view of about two dozen strangers, so he shrugged out of his coat and draped it over her torso for modesty's sake.

That earned him a dazzling smile from the bridesmaid. "How thoughtful."

A sunray slipped from behind a stray cloud and turned her light hair to spun silk, making it impossible for him to resist taking a good look at her, even though he hadn't intentionally looked past a woman's eyes for a year and a half. He discovered huge brown eyes, full pink lips and—dimples? Steeling himself against her cuteness, he looked away.

"Danielle isn't coming back," she whispered, "so there's no need to keep everyone."

"Right." He shifted to raise Miss Fannie's feet higher. Then he turned to look at the crowd. "The ambulance is on its way. We'll dismiss y'all so your cars won't block the drive."

The guests gathered their belongings and

started up the path to the house, consoling one another in low, solemn voices and whispers. Miss Fannie turned her head and watched them leave. "Jase," she whispered, "what about the bride?"

He glanced at the empty gazebo and around the estate. "No sign of her."

"She's flying home to Texas alone," the bridesmaid said.

"In all my years of hosting destination weddings, I've never had anything like—" Miss Fannie's bright blue eyes turned sorrowful. "I'm sorry, Jase. I wasn't thinking straight."

"No problem." He leaned over and patted her bony hand, catching a question in the bridesmaid's eye.

As the ambulance approached, inching across the fresh-mown lawn, the bridesmaid stood from her squatting position beside him. "I'm Erin Tucker. I'm sorry my flight arrived so late that we couldn't meet before the—before we started," she said, extending her hand. "And you're the Natchez Wedding Preacher."

Yeah, she looked like an Erin. Girl-next-door beauty, big, innocent eyes and a lilac scent like the first breaths of spring. Three good reasons to keep his distance and pretend he didn't see the pink-nailed hand she offered.

However, even after passing out on her lawn, Miss Fannie narrowed her eyes, her gaze boring into him in his hesitation. He was being rude, and he knew it.

"Jase Armstrong. Call me Jase." He reached up and took her hand, then quickly dropped it.

Because the Natchez Wedding Preacher knew how to keep a fresh-faced girl from shredding what was left of his heart.

Wouldn't you know, the first sweet, seemingly down-to-earth guy Erin had met in the past three years was a preacher.

A preacher who looked as if he'd just walked out of her favorite romance movie. But something about this minister—she wasn't sure what—set him apart from any actor she'd seen.

She watched him as the paramedics unloaded a stretcher, and suddenly she understood. It was his eyes, shining with so much love for Miss Fannie that Erin would have thought she was his grandmother if he hadn't called her by her first name.

Erin knew that expression. It was the look of a man who'd dedicated his life to the ministry, just like her father.

The lonely life Erin Tucker had vowed never to live.

It was a good thing she was leaving Natchez

tonight. Otherwise, she might have a hard time keeping her distance from this devastatingly handsome man—

She stopped the thought cold. Reverend Armstrong was probably married with a child or two at home. If he was, and if he prioritized ministry over the closest people in his life, as her former fiancé and her father had, she felt sorry for this preacher's wife and kids.

Nonetheless, Erin couldn't help checking his left hand for a ring—and found none.

She turned to see a golf cart rolling their way, decorated with pink azaleas. Erin smiled, anticipating meeting a woman who would deck out her quirky little vehicle with flowers. Within moments, the white-haired driver bounded out of the cart. About ten years younger than Miss Fannie, this lady rocked her raw-hemmed jeggings, long blue sweater and leopard-print flats.

"Fannie, what happened?" she asked when she reached the stretcher.

"I must have fainted." Miss Fannie held out her hand, which the other lady promptly took.

Jase cleared his throat, standing guard at the head of the stretcher while the paramedics strapped Miss Fannie in. "Eugenia Stratton, this is Erin Tucker, the bridesmaid. Miss Eugenia is my brother's grandmother-in-law and my dear friend."

"*Miss* Erin Tucker?" Miss Eugenia asked, leaning closer, eyes glistening.

"Yes, ma'am," she said.

Miss Eugenia's sly smile, aimed at the preacher, and raised brows meant something to Jase, judging from his suddenly downcast gaze and reddening neck.

"We're sending her to the hospital to find out why she passed out," he said.

"What brought you here, Eugenia?" Miss Fannie asked. "Did you know I had fallen?"

No, she hadn't merely fallen. There was more to her condition than that. But Erin chose to let that fact slide for now.

"I didn't know about your fall. I came to see the bride." She peered at her friend. "What happened, and where are you hurt?"

"I'm not. I just had a momentary spell."

"Thank the Lord for that," Miss Eugenia said. "I'll bring you a jar of kimchi when you get home. I just made a new batch. It'll perk you up in no time."

"Oh, good. And you're always welcome at a Rosewood wedding." This must be the Southern hospitality Erin had always heard about—offering neighborly kindness on your way to the hospital in an ambulance. As offbeat as it was, she kind of liked it.

With the older lady securely fastened onto

the stretcher, the paramedics loaded her into the ambulance.

"I'll meet you at the hospital, Miss Fannie," Jase said. "As soon as I lock up everything here."

While the ambulance inched across the lawn, Miss Eugenia took charge. "Go ahead to the hospital. I'll lock up." Then she glanced around the grounds. "Where is everybody? The bride and groom? The guests?"

Erin drew a deep breath, let it out slowly. "It…didn't work out. The bride, my college roommate, changed her mind at the last minute."

"She left her groom at the altar?" The older lady swiveled her head toward Jase so fast, she could have sprained her neck. "Oh, Jase, I'm sorry you had to see that."

What? The botched wedding certainly wasn't the preacher's fault…

"It's okay. Erin made things easier. She did a great job taking care of Miss Fannie."

"It wasn't a big deal," she said. "I'm a nurse, so it was mostly instinct."

"A nurse…" Miss Eugenia's eyes took on that same gleam they'd had earlier, when she'd basically asked if Erin was married. "Jase, take her with you to the hospital. She could be a big help. Can you go, Erin? Surely you don't have plans, since you thought you'd be here at the reception all evening."

Go along? With the preacher? Not if she could help it. Besides, Miss Eugenia seemed to be setting them up, and Erin didn't need that. "Miss Fannie won't want a stranger around since she isn't well."

"She likes you. I can tell. You'll be a comfort to her, especially since she has no family left. Some of the hospital staff will probably be strangers to her, too, so one more won't hurt." Miss Eugenia pointed in the direction of the garage. "Get moving!"

"Yes, ma'am." Jase grinned and glanced at Erin. "You okay with that?"

When Erin hesitated, he drew closer and dropped his voice to a whisper, his blue eyes twinkling, his charming smile dangerous. "To keep me out of trouble with Miss Eugenia?"

Oh, she shouldn't do it. "I'll look silly in a hospital ER, dressed like this."

"You'll just look like you're on a date," Miss Eugenia said as she climbed back into her golf cart and headed for the house.

Judging from the preacher's wide eyes, he didn't want a date any more than she did. Good. Then he wouldn't try to turn it into romance.

Besides, she was leaving Natchez tonight, and she'd surely never return.

Ten minutes later, Jase parked his Mustang in the one hospital parking spot marked for clergy. He came around and opened Erin's door, then took her hand and helped her out.

Wow, when was the last time a man had done that for her?

Working as a private nurse for some of New York's wealthiest people, she'd watched handsome men treat their dates like royalty, because some of them were. Since Erin usually stood on the sidelines, nearly invisible and blending in with the rest of the staff, she let herself enjoy the short-lived attention.

Thinking back, had any man ever made her feel special like this? Honestly, if she ignored her surroundings as they crossed the parking lot, she could almost imagine he was taking her to Paris's Tour d'Argent instead of a dated-looking small-town hospital the size of a clinic.

"My mom's working in the ER tonight, so she'll fill us in about Miss Fannie," Jase said as he opened the staff entrance door for Erin.

"She's a nurse?"

"Nurse practitioner. But it'll be up to me to convince Miss Fannie to follow Mama's orders, since I'm her power of attorney. I also manage her property and the destination weddings."

"It must be hard to have no living relatives."

He lowered his voice as they approached the

registration desk. "Her husband died of cancer fifty years ago. She doesn't have kids, and she never remarried."

"She has only you and Miss Eugenia."

"And a lot of other friends, especially in our church. Our senior pastor says we could call ourselves either a small church or a big family."

Finishing with the patient she'd been checking in, the ER receptionist motioned Jase to the window. Her face deeply lined and her sparse salt-and-pepper hair pulled back with a ponytail extension, she had the aura of a woman who'd held this department in line longer than Erin had been alive.

Jase headed straight for the receptionist's window. "Miss Jessie, can you tell Mama I'm here?"

In this small town's tiny hospital, the staff had probably been waiting for Jase to arrive.

"I called and told her as soon as I saw you drive up in that fancy car of yours." She pointed at the window wall and, sure enough, they could see Jase's Mustang in the clergy parking spot. Then, her deep brown eyes twinkling, Miss Jessie held her finger over her lips as she slid open a drawer, pulled out an oversize chocolate bar and pushed it through the little slit in the Plexiglas that was there for patients' insurance cards. Not for an elderly lady to sneak junk food to handsome young ministers.

Jase snatched up the chocolate and gave Miss Jessie a heartbreaking smile and a wink.

She laughed and waved him away.

Stepping from her domain, Jase motioned for Erin to follow and then unwrapped the candy bar.

What was he thinking? "Are you going to eat that here?"

He broke off a piece and held it out to Erin. "If I don't, I'll hurt her feelings. She keeps them there just for me."

"But we're in an ER. There's germs everywhere. You touched the door handles and—" Then she caught the compassion in his eyes.

"Sick people aren't the only ones in a hospital who need healing," he said in that deep-South accent of his that could melt the icing right off a three-tier wedding cake. "Miss Jessie's sixteen-year-old granddaughter just entered drug rehab. Giving helps Jessie's heart to heal."

Well, since he put it that way…

Erin took a bite, grinned and waved at Miss Jessie.

The woman's smile proved Jase was right. Apparently, the Wedding Preacher's calling didn't end with performing marriage ceremonies.

A swinging door opened across the hall from

them, and a slim blond lady approached, wearing her hair in a cute messy bun and a sleeveless lab jacket over her flowered poet top and straight black ankle pants. Her name badge indicated she was a nurse practitioner.

"Mama, this is Erin Tucker, the nurse who helped Miss Fannie when she fell," Jase said. "Erin, this is my mother, Anise Armstrong."

She hadn't expected such a youthful-looking woman, perhaps because Erin's mom had her later in life. Jase and Anise didn't look alike, either. Maybe Jase got his dark hair from his father.

"Looks like you're also the bridesmaid," Anise said, her gaze skimming Erin's pink dress. She gave Jase a bright—hopeful?—smile.

Erin resisted the urge to comment. Did everyone in Natchez want to marry Jase off? "Right. I'll probably just be in the way here, but Miss Eugenia insisted I come along. And this way, I get to tell Miss Fannie goodbye. I'm leaving Natchez tonight."

"Going home?" Anise asked.

How could Erin answer that? Might as well be honest. "I don't have a home."

She could feel their blank stares as she shifted her gaze to the polished tiled floor.

"Don't have... What do you mean?" Jase

said, his accent deepening. "Do you need help? Need a job? Because Mama can—"

"No, that's not it. I'm a private nurse for the elderly of the Hamptons. I live with my clients."

Anise nodded to Miss Jessie, who clicked open the door behind them. "So you took time off to attend your friend's wedding?" she said, leading them into the ER.

Erin should say yes and let it go at that. Otherwise, they'd ask more questions. But something about Jase's and Anise's concerned expressions wouldn't let her. "My client passed away on Sunday. I stayed for the funeral, and that's why I was nearly late for the wedding."

"But this is Saturday," Jase said as they approached the trauma rooms. "Did they delay the funeral that long?"

"I accompanied my client to Paris last fall. She died there, and I had to make arrangements, including booking a flight back to New York for myself. And the—body." She heard her voice breaking, her throat as tight as if she hadn't already cried a thousand tears for her elderly friend.

Miss Anise reached for Erin's hand. "I see how deeply you cared for her."

Erin swallowed hard, pushing down her grief. "I worked for and traveled with Mrs. Fairchild for two years and loved every minute. Not just because of the amazing sights we saw and events we attended. And the food…"

France had been her life, her passion. Mostly her escape. "I admit losing both Mrs. Fairchild and Paris in one afternoon took something out of me."

Then she stopped. "I'm sorry. We're here to talk about Miss Fannie, not me."

Jase's mom reached out and rubbed her back, a gentle touch that nearly brought tears to Erin's eyes. "Where will you go tonight? To your parents' home? Some other relative?"

Hardly. "I have a rental car waiting, and I'll find a hotel in Jackson tonight and fly to New York in the morning. I might book a condo in the Hamptons for two weeks or so while I find another job. Mrs. Fairchild and I spent summers in her home there."

But the Hamptons didn't hold the attraction it once had. Her only contacts in the area had been in Mrs. Fairchild's circle. Erin had no friends of her own there. Certainly no family. But she had to live somewhere until she found another job.

"Think about staying here instead," Anise said, stopping outside the closed door of a patient room and lowering her voice. "I'll discharge Miss Fannie in a few hours, but she can't stay home alone. She needs either a nursing home or a private nurse to keep her safe and monitor her meds."

Erin smiled, clearly seeing the direction Anise was going. "She'd hate a nursing home, wouldn't she?"

"That's for sure," Jase said.

Anise flashed a quick smile at her son, which made her look even younger and prettier. Then she turned back to Erin. "Would you consider staying in Natchez for a few weeks if Miss Fannie agrees?"

Erin could think of worse things than spending two winter weeks in warm southern Mississippi. But they'd have to make up their minds soon, because Miss Fannie had to go somewhere tonight—either home or to a nursing center.

How ironic that neither of them knew where they'd sleep tonight.

"I think that would work out, if she wants me. I'll just need to cancel my flight and car."

"Jase, what do you think?"

A fleeting hesitation crossed his face. Then he nodded. "I think it would be the best thing for Miss Fannie."

She half expected him to add, *but not for me*. Well, if the handsome preacher chose to distance himself from her during the next two weeks, it was all right with Erin.

"Great. Let's talk to Miss Fannie. And another thing…" Anise looked around behind her as if making sure no one was listening. "You should know that Jase is her estate manager and cook, and he also takes care of her wedding venue business. Miss Fannie lived alone at Rosewood the past fifty years, but about a year and a half ago, she decided that, at her age, she shouldn't live alone. So Jase moved into the third-floor apartment of her home. It's good for both of them."

Anise knocked and then opened the door. "It's me, Miss Fannie. Jase and the bridesmaid from the wedding are with me."

"Bring them in," Miss Fannie said from behind the curtain.

She shifted in the bed as Anise and Jase took positions on either side of it. That left Erin standing at the foot, gazing directly at the woman who might become her next client. A shadow of fear darkened Miss Fannie's eyes— fear of being sent to a nursing home and perhaps never coming home again, unless Erin missed her guess. She gave the elderly lady her warmest smile and waited for Anise to speak.

"Miss Fannie, I think I've found a nurse for you," Anise said in a calm, reassuring voice. "Erin is an experienced private nurse, and she has agreed to come live at your house for two weeks to help you get stronger."

The older lady held out both hands to Erin, even the one with an IV attached, and Erin moved closer and took them.

"This is an answer to my prayers. I wanted to go back to my own home." Miss Fannie squeezed her hands, her grip feeble, her eyes turning misty as the fear evaporated. "We'll turn the parlors into bedrooms for us until I'm better and can move back upstairs."

"I'm glad you'll be able to go home. Miss Fannie, let's talk about your care," Anise said, relief in her voice. At the older woman's nod, she continued. "You're dehydrated, as Erin suspected, so she'll see that you get plenty of fluids, and she'll watch your blood pressure and make sure you take your heart pills correctly. She'll also help you with the daily strengthening exercises physical therapy will order. And you'll need assistance to walk and do your personal care until your dizziness subsides and you're strong enough to walk alone."

"That sounds fine." Her voice thick with emotion, Miss Fannie turned to Erin. "Thank you, dear."

Anise's phone rang, and she stepped away to take the call.

"I brought my dog, Tasha, with me," Erin

told Miss Fannie. "The vet has her until to-night since I thought I'd be busy with the wedding and reception. Tasha is a Pembroke Welsh corgi. I don't know how you feel about dogs in the house—"

"I love dogs. I have a golden retriever named Sunny. Will Tasha get along with her?"

This arrangement was working out better than Erin had thought. "My former employer had a golden, and they were the best of friends. I'll need to pick up Tasha from the vet tonight."

"Is she at Dr. Thornton's animal clinic?" Jase asked. "If so, I'll arrange for one of the staff to deliver her to Rosewood. They do it for Sunny all the time."

"Yes, that's the place."

"Elinor Thornton is the women's ministry leader at our church. She does favors for us in return for Jase's chicken and dumplings," Miss Fannie said, a twinkle in her eye.

"Looks like it'll be the three of us for a while, Miss Fannie," Jase said.

Erin smiled. "Five, counting the dogs."

"We'll make it a house party like the ones you had when you were young." Jase shot Miss Fannie a grin that would endear him to any woman. "I'll pull out my best recipes. We'll eat like kings."

"And have pizza and popcorn when we feel

like it." Miss Fannie clapped her hands. "Sleep late in the mornings and play games every night."

Erin couldn't hold back a grin. "This sounds like the most pleasant job I've ever—"

She stopped when Anise stepped into the room, her face ashen.

Chapter Two

Jase had seen that expression on his mother's face only one other time: three years ago, when she'd learned her ex-husband—Jase's father—had died. Now Jase quick-stepped to his mother. "Mama? You okay?"

"That was Joseph Duncan on the phone. Our attorney," Anise said, casting a glance at Erin. Then she sank onto the straight-backed chair by the bedside. Drew a huge breath and set her gaze on her son. "He tried to call you."

Jase checked his phone, then held a button to turn up the volume. "I still had it silenced from the wedding. What's wrong?"

"It's Courtney."

"What? Is she all right? Is the baby okay?"

"She was taking Bella home from the hospital this afternoon, and a pickup hit them on the interstate." Mama swiped her fingertips under her eyes. "The baby wasn't hurt, but the truck T-boned the car on Courtney's side."

T-boned by a pickup? No, this couldn't be good...

She reached for his hand and squeezed hard. "Jase, she's gone."

He dropped his gaze to the floor. Hesitated. "She was so mixed up..."

"There's more. I want you to sit down." She got up from the chair, nudged Jase into it.

"Mama, you're scaring me. What's going on?" Judging from the tremor in Miss Fannie's lips and Erin's pale face, she was scaring them all.

"Before she...died, she told the doctor she was giving her baby to her favorite cousin." Her eyes turned even more sober. "Jase, Courtney named you the baby's guardian."

His heart lurched, and he wasn't sure if it started again or not. Guardian. Of a baby.

A bachelor with a baby. And that bachelor was him.

Jase rubbed his chest, hoping the friction would restart his heart. This wasn't just a baby, either. It was a newborn girl—what, two or three days old?

And this confirmed bachelor was expected to figure out how to feed her, change her, bathe her—raise her? Actually, Jase wasn't sure he'd even know how to keep her alive.

He slumped in the chair, unsure if his sudden weakness was from shock or the instant exhaustion taking over his limbs. Good thing Mama had asked him, no, *forced him*, to sit down.

"Jase, I'm sorry. I know how close you and Courtney were." Mama's gentle, shaky voice brought him back from the place of total panic he'd been heading toward.

"She was more than a cousin, even though she pretty much ignored me after she moved in with Craig and started living the party life with him last year. Even after he died, she hardly ever returned my calls or answered the door when I went to her apartment. I guess she felt guilty about the way she was living." His voice came out hoarse, raspy. In the grief that now settled on him like fog, his heart started behaving again. "Still, Courtney was always like a sister."

"I know. And at some point, you'll need to take time to grieve her." Mama reached over and pulled a tissue from the box on the table beside him. Dabbed the corners of her eyes and then her nose. "Did you know she had a will, and that she named you the baby's guardian and expressed her wish that you adopt her?"

Jase let his gaze drift to the window to the parking lot, catching sight of a woman buckling a baby into an SUV. "She told me when you and I went to the hospital to see Bella, but I never thought it would happen."

"Well, it looks like you need to leave for the Fayette hospital, because there's a baby there who needs her daddy."

"Get—get the baby now? Tonight?"

"As soon as you can. I'll call Joseph and try to set up an appointment with him for Monday morning, since you'll need legal advice about guardianship and adoption." His mother turned to Miss Fannie. "I'm sorry to conduct our family business in your hospital room. But you've always been family."

"And y'all to me." Miss Fannie turned her blue-eyed gaze to Jase. "Think you can tote a baby up and down two flights of stairs several times a day?"

His mind steered toward that panic spot again.

"Mama," he said, his chest tightening, "I can't take care of a baby. Give me a roomful of teenagers any day, but—"

"Jase, you're going to have to calm down." Mama used that unruffled voice she had, the one that could quiet frightened patients, unruly teens and even misbehaving dogs.

But what about babies? Jase didn't have a voice like that. And with this wild new responsibility he knew nothing about, he couldn't calm down. "I won't know what to do if the baby starts crying on the way home."

"Babies are going to cry," Erin said.

He turned toward her, caught the kindness in her voice, her eyes. Honestly, he'd forgotten she was here.

"That's why someone usually goes along when a new mom has to take her baby somewhere," she said. "The other person drives while the mom sits in back and takes care of the child. You'll need someone to sit in the back. I'd be glad to ride with you, as long as we'll be back in time for me to get Miss Fannie settled in at home."

"It's about a half hour each way. And possibly another hour for paperwork and a social services interview. You'll have to prove your identity, too." Mama tapped her fingers on her jaw—her thinking pose. "Miss Fannie, you'll be ready to leave the hospital in about an hour, but I don't get off duty until midnight. What if I ask Abe and Rosemary to take you home and stay with you? That way, Erin can go with Jase to get the baby."

Perfect solution. Miss Fannie loved Jase's big brother and his wife. And she'd enjoy spending time with their daughter, Georgia, too. "Miss Fannie? Would that be okay?"

"Fine. Just think—a baby in the house." Her eyes sparkled as she looked around the room. "Is there any paper in here? I want to make a list of the baby furniture you'll need from my attic. I've kept it stored there all these years. Ask Abe to find some strong young men to help, and they can bring it down tonight before you and the baby get home."

"Baby furniture—I hadn't thought of that," he said. "How much more baby stuff do I need?"

And not even know it? This was not going to work...

"Mama, I'm simply not the person for this job."

She pulled the room's rolling stool toward him, sat and faced him. "Jason, of all the people in the world, you're the one who can best raise this child. Courtney told the doctors that, besides your close relationship, she named you as guardian because we adopted you as a newborn, which means you'll know how to be this child's true family. And she was right. You'll know what Bella needs better than anyone. You can make her feel loved and cherished."

Oh, Mama... I learned it from you.

His eyes burned with memories of his mother's extra efforts to make him feel as loved as his older brother—his parents' natural son—especially when Dad's comments had made him feel second rate, less than, somehow damaged by the circumstances of his birth. Not as valuable as the child Dad had fathered. Not as important as Abe.

Not as loved.

Mama was right. He had to do this. Had to take this child.

But that didn't mean he understood how it was going to work.

"Okay. But who's going to take care of Bella while I'm managing Rosewood and working at church? Even I know the baby is too small to go to daycare."

The little room went quiet, as if its occupants focused all their energy on this problem. Which they probably were. Finally Erin broke the silence. "Miss Fannie, what if you and I take care of the baby together while Jase is at work? And we can give him lessons on baby care in the evenings. He'll have to find a babysitter once I'm gone, but this will give him time."

Seeing Miss Fannie's eyes soften with a tear, Jase suddenly understood another benefit of this arrangement. Including the older lady in the baby's care would mean the world to her,

since she had been denied the privilege of raising her own when her baby was stillborn.

"Yes, I can't wait to hear the sound of a baby
in my house," Miss Fannie whispered.

Thirty minutes later, Jase dropped Erin off
at Rosewood Cottage, the bride's suite near the
chapel, promising to retrieve her suitcase later.
Then he headed for the main house's kitchen
to check the whiteboard for messages. It was
wiped clean, but a note stood propped against
the wedding cake box.

Jase,
Your brother called and said they were
bringing Fannie home. There's enough
wedding-supper leftovers for them all in
the refrigerator, including a sack for you
and Erin to eat on the road. I'll come over
tonight to see the baby.
Eugenia Price Mabel Stratton

As always, she'd signed her full name, as if
anyone else named Eugenia would have been
here.

Sunny trotted in to greet him as he pulled
out the sack Miss Eugenia had packed, making
sure she'd put cake in it. After feeding the dog,
he hurried to his office in the rear wing, veri-
fied Erin's nursing license online and called her

references. Based on her previous employers' reports, she was a real treasure. That came as no surprise. She'd been great with Miss Fannie.

A knock sounded on the front door, followed by the familiar creaking of hinges.

"Jase?"

Erin. He got up and met her on the back gallery, the baby suddenly weighing heavy on his mind again, now that he'd finished his business calls. "I meant to pick you up, but the families you worked for wouldn't stop talking about you."

"I didn't mind walking."

"Come on inside the main house while I lock the front door."

His new employee smiled as she entered the center hall ahead of him, looking sweet in her pretty blue-and-white dress with a denim jacket and high-heeled sandals. As she skimmed past him, her lilac scent followed. "Glad my references checked out."

"Me, too. We're all set for you to start." He hesitated. "Unless you've changed your mind. You probably noticed Miss Fannie is a little on the eccentric side."

She smiled, and those dimples popped out again. "Seems there's a lot of that in Natchez."

Now that he thought of it, maybe so.

Erin gestured toward the west wall. "That looks like Zuber wallpaper."

How did she know that? "They say it's been here since 1834."

"I saw the same design in the White House once, when my former client was there to accept an award."

Miss Fannie would love that story. Erin was going to fit right in.

Later, after a shopping trip to Walmart and the half hour drive to Fayette, Jase turned off the car and glanced in the back seat. Usually crammed with teen boys, sports equipment or church supplies—or all three—his vehicle no longer looked like his. Erin had packed the diapers, clothes and who-knew-what-else in the trunk after their Walmart stop on the way to the hospital. But the back seat held the baby seat, diaper backpack and formula, and he wasn't completely sure Erin, even as slim as she was, would fit in there. He probably should have listened to Miss Fannie and taken her SUV.

Erin opened her door, but Jase hesitated, rubbing his hand across his eyes. "I haven't been this scared since I preached my first sermon."

The passenger door closed. He opened his eyes and chanced a glance at Erin.

She reached over and took his hand, her soft brown eyes gentle. "That's natural. Because the moment you carry the baby out of the hospital, your life will never be the same. Ever."

That much was sure.

"Truth is, I don't know anything about being a father. My dad left when I was small, and even when he was around, he wasn't much of a father. So, although my pastor and another family friend, Joseph Duncan, stepped in, I've never had a good example of how to be a father."

Erin paused, compassion in her beautiful eyes. "Do you mean your birth father left?"

He blew out a breath. "Actually, I was talking about my adoptive father. I never knew my birth parents because my natural mother gave me to Mama as soon as I was born. In fact, I know next to nothing about them."

"A lot of adoptions were closed back then. Maybe more than now."

"It wasn't closed, but Mama was friends with my natural mom, Starr, back when they lived in Nashville. Mama and Dad were married already, and all three of them were trying to break into the music business. My mother has the most beautiful soprano voice you'll ever hear. And my dad sounded like Elvis." Jase shut his eyes, recalling the little he knew about his birth parents. "Mama always said Starr asked her to keep her information secret because of her own past. I always got the idea that Mama didn't want me to find Starr. I didn't want to hurt Mama, so I didn't look for her."

"Was she afraid of your birth father?"

He shook his head. "Nothing like that. At least, not that I know of. But apparently, Starr lived the party lifestyle. She knew my mom didn't, and when my parents decided to leave Nashville behind and come home to Natchez, Starr wanted them to adopt me and give me what she thought would be a stable home."

"What about your birth father?"

"I don't know anything about him. So one father is a complete blank in my life. The other was an irresponsible man who took off with another woman, leaving us with a home fore-closure and a mountain of debt. But even while Dad was here, he was still the stereotypical irresponsible musician who would rather sit around playing music with the guys than spend time with his sons. This is why I know nothing about being a father." Jase chanced a glance at Erin to gauge her reaction to the strange cir-cumstances of his birth.

"Jase, I've known you only a few hours. But something about you—I'm not sure what it is, but it convinces me you can do this. I noticed it the moment you sat on the grass and let me lay Miss Fannie's feet on your knees." She held his gaze, an unwavering strength in her eyes that he hadn't noticed until now, one that made him think she did understand his fear, his self-doubt. One that had to have come from experience. "If you can love Miss Fannie that deeply, you'll be a fine father."

He swallowed hard, forced a smile. "Guess I have to. I'm all this baby has for a dad."

She hesitated. "Jase, I guess it's none of my business, but what happened to Bella's father?"

He drew a deep breath. "He died in a boating accident last fall. Boats and beer can be a dangerous combination."

Compassion welled in her eyes. "No grandparents, either?"

"Courtney's parents have been divorced for years. Her dad—my uncle—is in prison, and her mama—" He hesitated, not wanting to gossip but feeling Erin had a right to know. "Her name is Rita. She was convicted of child abuse and lost custody when Courtney was in kindergarten. Rita did some jail time, too. They haven't seen each other in eight years. Besides, last I heard, Rita had pretty bad emphysema, so she probably isn't healthy enough to take care of Bella, even if she was a fit grandmother. Which she isn't."

"Then I'm glad Bella has you." Erin let go of his hand. "Ready?"

He drew in a deep breath. Let it out. It was time.

After what seemed like hours of paperwork and the social services interview, Jase paced the room the staff had given them in the maternity unit. In a few seconds, a stranger would walk through that door and hand him a child who would be a part of him forever. This must be what Jesus's earthly father felt like before he saw Him for the first time. A baby who was not his child but who had been entrusted to him. *Lord, help me to have Joseph's faithfulness as I try to raise this baby.*

"How long have we been in here? It feels like an hour." He glanced at the door.

Erin looked at her watch, a smile twitching on her lips. "Ten minutes."

Realizing how annoying his pacing probably was, he crossed the room for the hundredth time and flopped down on the fake-leather couch by the window. "I'm going to be a terrible student. You have your work cut out for me, teaching me how to take care—"

After a light knock, the door swung open to reveal a nurse in blue scrubs, about Miss Eugenia's age, holding a tiny bundle in a pink blanket.

Jase was across the room before he realized he'd stood. He looked down at the small face for an instant.Then it began to blur. Was it his imagination, or was this baby a miniature Courtney? He hadn't noticed the resemblance when he and Mama had come to see her a couple days ago.

He tensed his jaw, grief hitting him in the chest and knocking the breath from him. He swiped at his eyes, swallowed back the pain that wanted to crawl from his throat and escape in a howl.

Courtney...

He'd succeeded in pushing his cousin from his mind all day, determined to delay his grief until he was alone. But now the memory of her jaunty smile and teasing voice wouldn't leave him. And she'd thought of him in her last moments, remembered the closeness that had made them more like siblings than cousins.

And she'd given him her child.

Something shifted in him then as sudden clarity dropped into his heart—a clarity he couldn't define but one that changed everything he'd felt and everything he'd been up to this moment.

The nurse checked the wristband they'd given him, and then he reached for the sleeping baby girl and cradled her in his arms, unashamed of his grief as he embraced this gift. When his tear landed on her face, the baby opened her eyes. Blue, like Courtney's. She fixed her tiny gaze on him. Opened her mouth, gave a shuddering gasp, as if sorrowing with him.

He passed his hand over her dark hair then touched her little fist as it batted the air. She reached for his finger, her big eyes still focused on him.

She smacked her lips and closed her eyes, falling into instant sleep, the biggest part of his heart now wrapped around those tiny fingers that held his, helpless, trusting. Trusting him, even in slumber.

"Oh, little one, as God is my witness, I will be your daddy, your provider, your protector— it'll be you and me, baby girl, for the rest of my life."

Yes, this was surely how Joseph had felt.

Erin reached for a tissue from the box on the table, unwilling to break this moment, and dabbed her eyes. If she'd had doubts about this arrangement, they disappeared now as she took in Jase's glistening eyes and low voice, speaking words of love to the baby.

"I've worked on this floor for forty years, and I've never seen a baby take to a man this way," the nurse said, wiping her eyes. "Bella knows you're someone special."

Bella—Courtney had chosen the perfect name for this tiny girl.

Jase dragged his gaze from Bella to the nurse. "I don't know much about babies—yet. But she seems so little."

"She came a few weeks early, but she's fine." The nurse looked around the room, gestured at the diaper backpack and car seat on the table. "You have her home instructions, and you've signed her discharge forms, so if you want, you can go ahead and fasten her into her seat. Social services will be here shortly to do another interview, this time with the baby present. Then you'll be free to go."

But they were missing something. Some instruction, some precaution lurked in Erin's subconscious, too deep for her to retrieve. When the answer didn't come, she took a step toward the table, in case Jase wanted her to help.

She'd need to think about this later.

He moved to set the infant in the seat but hesitated, still holding Bella with both arms. "Um, how does this work?"

His charming helplessness touched Erin's heart. "Put one hand under her head, the other under her bottom. Just take it slow. You won't drop her."

"I've never held a baby this small before."
After a few moments of maneuvering, he managed to get her settled in the seat. He straightened and let out a victory grunt, making Erin laugh.

The first of many triumphs, she was sure.

When the social worker got there, Erin excused herself and stepped into the hallway. She pulled her phone from her purse and checked the time. Maybe she could catch Danielle, since her plane was supposed to land at six. She dialed her friend's number.

"I don't want to talk about Robert or the wedding," Danielle said without so much as a hello.

Well, okay. "Just checking to make sure you're all right."

"I'm not, and I might never be." The fake nonchalance in Danielle's voice grated against Erin's ears. "I'm in the baggage-claim area, looking for an empty suitcase."

What? "Empty?"

"The one that had my wedding dress in it. The dress that's along the side of the road somewhere between the Natchez city limits and the airport."

Oh. That suitcase.

"Where are you? Back in New York?" Danielle asked.

"No, I'm still in Natchez—"

"I see my bags, so I have to run," Danielle interrupted. "But stay away from that handsome preacher. I saw the way he looked at you."

"Don't worry. I won't make that mistake again."

"I'm not so sure. When you first got engaged to Calum, you said he wasn't like your dad, always putting ministry ahead of you. But they both skipped out on the most important day of your life, and you know why."

Erin sure did. It was because they had a chance to go and pray with somebody. And because ministry was more important than she was. That would never change.

"You were over-the-top in love with that man, and you've never gotten over him, Erin. Remember that when the wedding preacher turns on the charm and asks you out. Because it's probably going to happen. I can tell. So get out of Natchez as fast as you can."

Danielle was right about Calum and Erin's previous feelings toward him. However, she'd been over him for a long time. "But I promised to—"

"Gotta grab my stuff. I'll call you later."

No, she wouldn't. Erin ended the call, but she couldn't shake the conversation from her mind. And Danielle wouldn't call her back, because she never did. Their college days, plus the three years they'd spent working private nurse gigs, proved that Danielle lived completely in the moment, thinking of no one except the people in the room with her.

No wonder she couldn't marry Robert.

But when Jase came out of the room, carrying Bella in her car seat, Erin steeled her heart against the kind, sweet—and yes, handsome—man. Because she'd learned long ago that Danielle's rather dicey childhood had taught her a defense mechanism: discerning men's intentions. And even though Erin never wanted to be as cynical as Danielle, she had to admit her friend was right about one thing: where preachers were concerned, she'd always take a back seat to the ministry.

Thirty minutes later, Erin and Jase pulled into Rosewood's drive and parked beside several vehicles, including a flower-bedecked golf cart. Erin hurried out to assist Jase if he needed it. But he bundled the baby against the damp February breeze and carried her into the house himself.

As she followed him up the front steps and across the wide porch, she couldn't help thinking about that pivotal moment in the hospital, when Jase's demeanor had changed. The little six-pound baby, her sweet face all eyes, would capture anyone's heart. But Erin had rarely seen a man so awed by a newborn not his own.

Inside Rosewood's center hall, deep voices and laughter upstairs mingled with the sound of a little girl's chatter and a nearby thud on this level, as if a heavy object had landed on the wooden floor. Apparently, Jase's brother and his crew were here, carrying baby furniture downstairs.

At the sound of paws on the winding, carpeted stairs, Erin bent down and held out her arms to Tasha. After a brief hug, the corgi broke free and ran away with Sunny. "She didn't miss me much."

Jase laughed. "Sunny is the best hostess in the world. She makes friends with every dog who visits Rosewood, and this is always the result. But what happened to Tasha's leg?"

"She was born with only three. But she's never seemed to miss the fourth one," Erin said as the corgi raced down the hall.

As they moved farther into the hall, which was more like a big room in the center of the house, the aromas of Cajun seafood and grilled meat wafted toward her. Her stomach suddenly growling, she realized their bagged lunch of bacon-wrapped shrimp with cheeses, flatbreads and cake, eaten in the car on the way to the hospital, had been her only meal today.

Following Jase, who headed toward the voices, Erin prepared herself for introductions. This client seemed different than her others, who'd demanded proper social graces at every gathering. Not to mention staying on the correct side of the fine line of familiarity. All successful private nurses knew how close to get to their clients and their relatives. Her first client had demanded formality, distance. Mrs. Fairchild had wanted a grandmother-granddaughter-style relationship. This gathering would reveal Miss Fannie's preference.

"We're home," he called.

"Uncle Jase!" Amid barking from the two dogs, fast, light footsteps sounded from within a room down the hall. A little girl of about four, her dark curls caught up in a high ponytail, ran toward Jase, arms outstretched. Seeing the baby, she stopped, dropped her arms and took a step back, her eyes never leaving Bella.

"Hey, Georgia." Instantly Jase went down on one knee and held out his free hand to the girl. "Look what I have. This is your new cousin, Bella."

She inched closer, tried to sit on Jase's knee, but the baby was in the way. Her big blue eyes clouded. "Whose baby is she?"

"She's mine. I'm her daddy." His words

sounded a little strained, as if it would take him a while to get used to them.

"No," Georgia said, her voice wavering. "No, I'm your girl. Remember?"

Jase's wide eyes told Erin that he hadn't thought of this complication. She held out her arms. "I can take Bella," she said, glancing pointedly at his niece. "That way, she can share you with Georgia."

He flashed her a smile of thanks as she reached for the baby. Georgia hesitated a moment then flung herself at Jase. He picked her up and swung her around, drawing gales of laughter.

When he set her down, she looked at Erin and the baby. "Are you her mama?"

Her sweet Southern drawl tugged at Erin's heart. "No, but I'm going to help your uncle take care of her."

Georgia threw her arms around Erin's legs in a little-girl hug. "We came over to help Miss Fannie because she's going to get a nurse."

She hugged the child back with her free arm. The sudden tightness in her throat made her realize she missed her first job in the maternity unit. "I'm the nurse. Would you like me to teach you how to take care of Bella?"

"Uh-huh...yes, ma'am," she said, as if correcting herself.

As Georgia released her hold on Erin and ran after the dogs, Miss Eugenia came down the winding staircase and into the hall like she was on a mission, her stylish flats clattering against the wooden treads. She stopped long enough to see Bella before heading down the hall, the dogs reappearing from who-knew-where and following. "Fannie's in the ladies' parlor. She finally agreed to let us move out some of the relics in there to make room for her bedroom furniture. And don't pass the baby around. She's too young."

Pass the baby...

That was it. The nugget of information Erin tried to remember since they left the hospital. She watched Georgia follow her great-grandmother down the hall, recalling the "caring for adopted babies" section of her pediatrics class. "Miss Eugenia is right, Jase, but not only because of germs. Adopted newborns need to bond with just the new parents at first instead of being held by a bunch of different people."

"That makes sense." But the concern in the blue depths of his eyes told her he realized that one parent, working two jobs, couldn't do that. "How much do we have to limit other people?"

"Maybe let your family members hold her briefly, no more than one per day. And of course, Miss Fannie and I will hold her, too."

But what would happen if Bella began to bond with Erin? Would the baby miss her when she was gone?

"We don't have a choice, but it's not ideal, especially since you're leaving soon," Jase said, as if he'd guessed her thoughts.

"Agreed."

When they reached the threshold of the parlor-turned-bedroom, Erin took in the mishmash of ornate Victorian sofas and chairs, a bedroom suite that might have seen the Mexican-American War, and a case clock in the corner. Miss Fannie lay on a red velvet daybed by the jib window, directing two young men who carried in a highboy dresser. Pocket doors, pulled halfway out, divided the room. Erin realized the men were delivering the dresser to her new bedroom.

"There's my girl," Miss Fannie called, dressed in a flowing light blue skirt and a long white tunic and looking like the lady of the manor that she was.

Erin crossed the spacious room to Miss Fannie's side. A quick nursing assessment revealed pinker cheeks and brighter eyes. Good signs. "This is Bella. Do you feel well enough to hold her?"

"Of course." Miss Fannie reached for the sleeping baby, her eyes filling.

Something felt so right about her boss's involvement in the baby's care.

After a moment, Miss Fannie pulled her gaze from the child and glanced around the room, her lids fluttering as if blinking back tears. "The baby furniture is in your apartment, Jase. Now we're moving furniture down from the second floor—from my room and the best guest room—until I can climb the stairs." She turned to Erin. "Feel free to ask the men to rearrange things to your liking," she said in a near-whisper. "Abe and Rosemary probably didn't hear you arrive. They're in the kitchen, heating wedding leftovers for supper."

"I'll get them. They'll want to see Bella." Jase headed for the hall. "Besides, I need to supervise. Rosemary can cook, but not with Abe in the kitchen. He has the bad habit of throwing a ton of curry powder and turmeric into everything."

"Even my grandmother's corn pudding recipe," Miss Fannie said when he'd gone. "But Jase can cook. His jambalaya is so good, it can make you cry."

A preacher who could cook, an estate manager with enough heart to raise an orphan baby, the Wedding Preacher who was now a single dad—was there anything Jase couldn't do?

Not to mention those big blue eyes that could look right through her…

She stopped the thought cold. Not only was she leaving town in two weeks, but he was in the ministry.

Two great reasons to keep her distance from Reverend Jase Armstrong.

Chapter Three

Jase had barely rescued the shrimp and grits from Abe's heavy-handed spice attack when a new assault came, this one hitting his ears from the direction of the parlor-bedroom.

It had to be Bella. But who knew a six-pound baby could cry that loud? And why so shrill? "Something's wrong with the baby."

His heart now racing, he dropped the long-handled serving spoon—the one he'd been threatening his brother with every time Abe made a move for the stove—and took off at a run for Miss Fannie's new room.

"Wait, Jase." He heard Rosemary's voice behind him. "All babies cry like that. It's natural."

He slowed his pace. Having been a mother for four years now, Rosemary should know. And Bella had slept during the ride home, so he didn't yet know her cry. Still… "It sounded like she fell off Miss Fannie's daybed or some-thing."

Erin met them at the parlor's doorway, a baby bottle in her hands. "What's wrong?"

Jase stopped so fast, he lost his balance for a moment and came close to slamming into her. "That's what I wanted to know. What's wrong with Bella?"

"She's just hungry. Did anything happen in the kitchen?" Erin laid her hand on his arm, somehow steadying him emotionally as well as physically, concern in her beautiful brown eyes. "I heard you pounding up the hall and thought maybe somebody got cut."

He groaned inwardly. Nope, it was just his old habit kicking in again. One of these days, he had to learn to stop fearing the worst every time anything went wrong. Although his life had kind of taught him to do that...

"The kitchen's fine. I managed to keep Abe from sabotaging supper."

Her soft smile somehow calmed his nerves a little. She held up the bottle in her hand. "Want to learn how to feed Bella?"

"Sure. As long as teaching me won't slow the process. Sounds like she wants it now."

"Which way is the kitchen?" she asked. "I'll show you how to make her bottle."

First he had to see that the baby was okay. He

stuck his head in the room. Sure enough, there sat Miss Fannie on her old-fashioned couch, holding Bella and making little noises to soothe her. Sunny and Tasha lay on the floor next to them, as if guarding both the elderly lady and the baby.

With his pulse slowing to a more normal rate now, he led Erin back to the kitchen. There he mock frowned at the small crowd gathered there, most of them smirking at his reaction to Bella's not-so-polite request for food.

Jase made quick introductions as Erin washed the bottle.

Banned from the stove, his brother, Abe, stood at the refrigerator instead, pulling out soft drinks along with a juice box for little Georgia. Dressed in camo pants and a close-fitting black T-shirt, he showed off his impressive biceps and pecs.

Abe's wife, Rosemary, the best cook in the family other than Mama, tested the reheating coq au vin. She wore her old I'm Just a Muffaletta T-shirt, her unborn baby beginning to show under it. Four-year-old Georgia hung around Abe, looking cute in her flowered denim jumper and pink shirt. As always, Rosemary's presence brought a sense of peace, of calm. Jase dared to hope Bella would pick up on that.

Off to the side stood thirteen-year-old Darnell Covington, trying to fit in but probably still not feeling it even after a year in Jase's youth ministry. At least now the long-legged redhead had a new foster family who seemed more suited to him, after the previous two hadn't worked out. Jase stepped over and gave him a brotherly punch on the arm. "Know anything about babies?"

He nodded. "My second foster family had a one-year-old and a two-year-old."

"Good," Jase said. "I need all the teachers I can get."

"Erin, I boiled some water ahead of time so it would be cool when you need it," Rosemary said, carrying over a covered pan from the counter.

"Great thinking. Lesson number one—warming the bottle." Erin's dimples showed again as she gave him a wide smile.

Jase averted his eyes from them, something he'd probably do a lot of for the next two weeks.

"Maybe you'd rather do the teaching, Rosemary," Erin said. "I've taken care of lots of babies, since my first job was in maternity. But you still have more experience than I do."

"No, I'll have plenty of time for bottles before long." Rosemary laid her hand on her abdomen.

"Okay then, class is in session." Erin turned to Jase. "Could you get out an older dish towel to use as a burp cloth until I can throw Bella's in the washer?"

He reached into the drawer beside the sink and found a faded blue one.

Light footsteps sounded in the hall, although Jase could barely hear them over the baby, who continued to protest the delay. Miss Eugenia stuck her head in the kitchen and glanced around, then gazed at Jase and Erin together at the counter. She hesitated. "Rosemary, I need you in the parlor. Or the bedroom, or whatever we're calling it now."

"Now, Grannie?"

"Right this minute. Abe, Darnell, we also need your muscles upstairs."

Jase knew that tight-lipped smile of hers. It meant she intended to get her way.

"We moved all the furniture, Miss Eugenia," Abe said, lounging against the wall with Darnell. "What else do you need?"

"Do as I say, Abe."

At the crook of the older lady's finger, Abe and Darnell followed her out the door. Passing by Jase, Darnell stopped, a hint of dejection in his eyes. "I guess we're not going to test your new recipe tonight, huh?"

Recipe. Jase groaned inwardly. How could

he have forgotten? "You're welcome to hang around tonight, but I think I'll have my hands too full to cook. But come over tomorrow after church for wedding leftovers, and we'll make pizza in the evening."

Darnell grinned and held up his hand for a high five. Jase gave it a good slap as the boy sprinted out, presumably to catch up with Abe.

Rosemary laughed as she followed her grandmother. "Watch out. That gleam in Grannie's eye means she smells romance. I don't think she knows you're leaving in two weeks, Erin."

But Miss Eugenia did know Jase was unavailable for romance. She'd been there for both of his attempted weddings. And she knew both of his fiancées had backed out because they didn't want a minister for a husband. Not to mention that no woman ever wanted him for who he was. Instead, they'd tried to talk him out of his calling.

Jase wished he dared to ask Rosemary if her grandmother was the famed mysterious matchmaker the whole town had speculated about for the past sixty years. Once, when he'd walked in on a conversation between Miss Fannie and Miss Eugenia at Rosewood, he'd heard hushed words that made him think Miss Eugenia had matched Miss Fannie to Colonel Chester, whom she'd sneaked off to marry. Whoever the matchmaker was, she must make the couples swear to keep her identity secret. Regardless, if she was trying to fix him up with Erin, she'd be disappointed.

Sorry, Miss Eugenia. Your romance radar failed this time.

Erin handed him the bottle, filled with what looked like a ridiculously small amount of milk. They reached the parlor-bedroom just as Miss Eugenia and Rosemary headed back to the kitchen. Erin sat in a nearby armchair, clearly leaving the daybed for him to sit by Miss Fannie. She laid the towel over his shoulder.

Jase took the baby and held her close to his chest. He reached for the bottle, then hesitated. Was it as simple as sticking it in her mouth? For some reason, he thought he should know more about the process than he did. But how could he, since the closest he'd ever been to a brand-new baby was looking on from a distance when a church family had a new addition? He'd never even conducted a baby dedication before. Pastor David always did that. And neither Jase nor Abe had seen Georgia until she was three.

"Keep her propped up, then tell her it's meal-time by brushing your finger lightly over her cheek. It'll make her turn her head toward the bottle," Erin said. "When you feed her, make sure there's no air in the nipple, so she doesn't get gas in her stomach."

"Here's your bottle, little Bella." Jase did as she said, and sure enough, when he touched Bella's cheek, she turned her head. He angled the bottle and she took it, making sweet little baby noises.

Soon Erin leaned in and looked at the bottle. "She's halfway done, so it's time to burp her."

Okay, he'd heard of the concept of burping a baby before...

"Take the bottle out of her mouth, hold her on your shoulder and gently rub her back." He didn't have to look at Erin to know she was grinning. He could hear it in her voice. "That's all there is to it."

Right. He pulled out the bottle, then maneuvered Bella around and up, sweat breaking out on his scalp. Resisting the urge to wipe it away, he tried to concentrate. He could do this. He just needed to focus—

He must have had a panicked expression, because Miss Fannie broke out in a giggle. "Relax, Jase. Even I can do it. You'll be fine."

"Sure, as long as I don't drop the baby. Or drown her in milk. Or forget to burp her—" He shot his gaze toward Erin. "What if I forget to burp her?"

"She'll remind you. She'll cry."

Great. He forgets one little thing and it'll make Bella cry? He'd been right. He was not the man for this job. This was going to be a disaster. "Look, when I said I have no idea how to take care of a baby, I wasn't exaggerating. I know absolutely nothing—"

"Jase." Something in Erin's calm, confident voice, the trust in her eyes, stopped his panic. "The fact that you're concerned about doing it right proves you will. I'd be worried if you weren't trying to learn or thought you could do it when you don't know how."

She might be right, but it didn't mean he felt any better.

"Taking care of an infant is half learned knowledge and half instinct and common sense." Erin stood and took the baby and the burping cloth from him. "We should have demonstrated first. Miss Fannie, since you know how, do you want to show him?"

Jase hated to admit he was glad to have someone else burp Bella this first time. But as soon as she left his arms, the warmth from her tiny body left, too. To his surprise, he missed it.

After Miss Fannie extracted a little burp from the baby, Jase fed her the rest of the bottle. Then, wonder of wonders, he coaxed another bit of air from her.

"You did a great job," Erin said, and Jase wasn't sure if he heard hesitation in her voice.

Maybe he hadn't done a great job. Until tonight, all he'd known about taking care of a baby was which end of the bottle went in her mouth, so how would he know?

Erin picked up Bella and carried her to the cradle. Then she knelt beside it and started taking off the little garment she had called a sleeper. "You've had enough learning for tonight. I'll change her diaper. We'll save that lesson for later."

Diapers. How many more lessons would he need? A hundred wouldn't be enough. And as Rosemary had said, Erin would be here only two weeks.

What would he do after that? Sure, he could call his mom or Rosemary if he needed help or advice. But what if something happened in the middle of the night? He couldn't exactly disrupt their sleep just because he didn't know what he was doing.

No doubt about it—Courtney's big idea of letting her bachelor cousin raise her baby was going to end in disaster.

In the two years Erin worked in New York's Lenox Hill Hospital, she'd seen probably twenty new dads unravel at the birth of their children. Jase was speeding in that direction.

It was time for an intervention.

Erin finished diapering the baby, who promptly fell asleep in the cradle, and then stood and crossed the room to Miss Fannie. "Are you feeling well enough for Jase and me to take a short walk if I get Miss Eugenia to sit with you?"

Miss Fannie glanced at the case clock. "I was thinking of asking for a tray in my room and turning in after supper."

That would work just as well. "Jase, would you excuse us while I help her undress? Maybe meet me in the kitchen in fifteen minutes?"

She could hear Abe and Rosemary, back in the kitchen, rattling around in there and getting dinner ready, so they'd distract Jase until Erin finished with Miss Fannie.

However, Erin had barely finished taking her vital signs when someone knocked on the door. "It's me, Fannie."

"Come in, Eugenia."

As Erin documented her patient's blood pressure, temperature, pulse and respirations in the notebook she'd bought, Miss Eugenia came in, carrying a loaded silver tray. Sunny stood to check it out and then lay down again. "I brought supper for us, and I'll help you get ready for bed when we've finished."

Erin stowed the blood pressure cuff, stethoscope, notebook and pen in the armoire. "Of course you're welcome to have dinner with her. But I'll help her get ready for the evening, in case she has another dizzy spell."

"No, I'll do it." Miss Eugenia smiled that tight-lipped smile Erin had seen earlier. The one that clearly meant she intended to have her way. But Erin couldn't let her do that unless her patient insisted.

"Miss Fannie, what would you like me to do?" she asked in the deferential tone she'd learned on her first day as a private nurse.

As her patient opened her mouth, Miss Eugenia spoke up. "Remember, Fannie, what I did for you and Chester back in 1969?"

"You mean when you were our match—"

"Yes, yes, that's it," Miss Eugenia interrupted, nearly shouting the words. "When I took you to New Orleans to meet Chester."

Understanding dawned on Miss Fannie's face. "Oh, you're trying to…yes. Yes, I would like you to eat with me and help me get ready for bed so Jase and Erin can take their walk."

These two had something up their sleeves, that was for sure. "Fine, but Miss Eugenia, please just lay out her nightclothes and don't try to help her to stand. I'll take her into the bathroom for her evening routine when she's ready, because we don't want her to fall."

"Of course. Just scoot along," Miss Fannie said. "Jase is in the kitchen."

When Miss Eugenia turned her back and began fussing with the tray, Miss Fannie smiled and waved Erin away.

She obeyed and headed first to her room to send a quick text to Danielle, who replied that she'd landed in Dallas and was spending time with her mom, just as she'd said she would. Then Erin hurried to the kitchen. There she found Jase with his back to her, leaning over the island's quartz countertop, in deep, quiet conversation with Darnell.

"I'm trying to trust Rick and Erica. I know they're good people," Darnell said, his voice cracking. "It's just hard to forget…you know… what my dad did—"

Jase rounded the island in a flash, wrapped his arm around the boy's neck and pulled him against him, giving him a manly hug. "Dude, I know. I know how it feels when your dad walks out."

Darnell broke down in tears then, his sobs loud and jagged, as Jase held the boy's head against his chest.

Erin crept from the doorway and outside to

the courtyard, her own eyes damp with unshed tears. Although she'd rewrite her whole childhood if she could, Darnell's sounded worse than hers. She wandered around the herb garden, then headed toward the vine-covered pergola and sat on one of the cold stone benches underneath.

Then she remembered Jase's words. His home life clearly hadn't been great, but she couldn't imagine life with Anise as his mom being all bad.

And the way he'd been there for Darnell—wow. Tonight, when everyone was taken care of and she was alone, in those quiet night hours when the past sometimes seemed almost like the present, and she relived her own similar memories, she'd need to keep her guard up. Because something about Jase, as he ministered to Darnell, reminded her far too much of another man. One who held the hearts of young people across the country. One who brought the gospel to crowds of hurting teens.

One whose heart Erin had broken.

The sun dropped low in the west, so she walked to the little chapel to warm up. Passing the gazebo, where Danielle had run, she heard Jase calling her name. She stopped and waved, then started back toward him, running her hands over her chilled arms.

When he reached her, he handed her an old-fashioned white sweater, the evening breeze blowing his hair a little. "Miss Fannie sent this. After sunset, it gets chilly and damp out here in February."

"How did she know I was here?"

"Trust me, she knows everything that goes on at Rosewood."

"I'm not surprised." Erin slid her arms into the softness of the hand-knit sweater. "I'm sorry I walked in on your private conversation with Darnell. I sneaked out as quietly as I could."

"He must not have known you were there, because I didn't." Jase started up the path, and she kept pace with him. "Look, I'm sorry to be such a slow learner about all this baby stuff. That has to be frustrating for you."

She shook her head. "It's not. I've taught a lot of new dads how to care for their newborns. It's harder for you, since you've never been around babies much and haven't been preparing throughout the pregnancy. Most men have, at least to some extent."

"I'm better with teens."

Yes. "I saw how great you were with Darnell. There's no reason you can't learn to take care of Bella, too." She had to ask the question that had hovered in her mind since they returned from the hospital. "Didn't you ever hold your niece or babysit her?"

"Nope. She lived in St. Simon's Island, in Georgia, with Rosemary until she was three." Jase pointed in the direction of the nearby gazebo. "Are you warm enough to sit in there for a few minutes? You're probably worn out, and I know I could use a rest."

"Sure. So Georgia lived in Georgia," she said. "And they never came home to see you and your mother, or Rosemary's grandmother?"

"Never." He drew a deep breath, blew it out slowly as if this was a long story. At the gazebo, they took a seat, sheltered a bit from the light wind. "See, they got married when they were twenty, but they didn't tell anyone. Two weeks after their secret wedding, they had an argument. Abe stormed out and joined the army, and Rosemary went to St. Simon's Island when she found out she was pregnant. Nobody in Natchez knew Georgia existed, except Rosemary's parents and grandmother."

Erin never would have guessed that. "Still, even without experience, you'll be a great dad. You have what it takes."

"Oh, yeah?" He said the words with a grunt, clearly not buying it. "What's that?"

She paused, weighing her words. "I don't know if it's an instinct or a ministry anointing, but you always know what people need. I saw it when Miss Fannie passed out. Then I saw it with Miss Jessie, the ER receptionist. And now again with Darnell. He must be okay now, since you're out here alone."

"He's fine. He's upstairs in my apartment, helping Abe and Rosemary organize the baby furniture chaos."

"That proves you have what it takes to care for people's needs. Rely on that, and you and Bella will be fine."

In the waning light, she saw the moment he got it.

He slowly nodded. "It's not anything I was smart enough to learn. The Lord did that for me to prepare me for ministry."

"And to prepare you to take care of Bella."

"Yes." His deep blue eyes turned to liquid in the sun's gold evening rays. "I can see it."

Erin stood to head back to the house, her task done, her intervention successful. And in two weeks, she'd wrap up this job and head back to the Hamptons. Or maybe back to Europe.

The only problem was, she had a feeling she'd see motherless Bella's sweet little face in her dreams for a long time to come.

It wasn't every day a single River Church pastor showed up for Sunday service with his newborn baby. Especially when no one in the congregation, other than his family and lead pastor, knew she existed.

If the Lord chose to answer Jase's early-morning prayers, the changes in his household wouldn't draw attention from the worship.

Pulling into the church parking lot, Jase rubbed his eyes. If he'd known Bella would wake up to eat every two hours during the night, he probably wouldn't have sat up working on the youth Valentine's Day program until midnight.

Lesson learned.

At least he'd had lots of opportunities to practice Erin's late-night teaching on diapers.

His baby—*his baby*—made a cute little snuffling noise in the back seat as Jase stopped the car and got out. Jase reached for the diaper backpack, loaded up with formula and other baby paraphernalia, and slipped his arms through the straps. Then he unfastened the car seat and headed toward the entrance with Bella.

If he'd thought he'd get to the door without the entire congregation swarming him and Bella, he'd been wrong. In fact, it looked like everyone who had ever attended River Church was here this morning. And the first ones to reach him were the last ones he'd have wanted:

a mob of single women, all with diamonds in their eyes.

Well, it might have been only three, but it seemed like a mob, crowding him and asking questions as he tried to maneuver the car seat into the building. Jase kept moving while answering them, hoping they'd take the hint and let him pass. Yes, this was his baby. No, he didn't have a secret wife like Abe had. And no, thank you, he didn't need help taking care of the baby, but if he ever needed their assistance, he'd let them know.

The crowd around him grew quickly, with families getting out of their cars, the women rushing him while the men got out of the way and meandered inside. Then the church door opened, and even more ladies streamed out from the foyer. The older ones were probably there to find out why their bachelor youth pastor was dodging the gawkers, trying to get a baby inside. The younger ones—who knew?

Why hadn't someone invented a less awkward car seat that could maneuver around a gang of unruly church women?

It didn't help that, without warning, Bella chose that moment to let out her earsplitting, heart-stopping cry.

Now what was he supposed to do? Jase had fed her then tried to burp her without success, but Miss Fannie had gotten air out of her and said it was enough. He'd thought Bella would just sleep until church was over. But no, she clenched her little fists and cried as if Jase had broken her heart.

He hadn't, had he?

And now the mamas and grandmas pushed through the crowd of the younger ones, and he had to answer the same questions all over again. Then their take-charge voices clamored as each tried to talk over the others.

"That's a hungry cry if I ever heard one."

"No, I think she's cold. Do you have another blanket with you, Pastor Jase?"

"It's too soon to bring her out in public. You should have left her home until she was six weeks old."

"Maybe something's sticking her. That's what my mother used to say when a baby wouldn't stop crying."

"No, I'm sure she's colicky."

Colicky? He'd heard of that, and just the mention of the word always seemed to send women into a state of panic. How would he know if Bella was colicky? What did the word mean, anyway?

He glanced around for Mama. Where was she when he needed her?

If his mother had known he was bringing

the baby to church by himself, she probably would have come early to help. But no, Jase hadn't called her, hadn't told her his plan to have his child in church on her first Sunday. Maybe he'd subconsciously withheld that bit of information, not wanting Mama to douse his plan. Erin had said it might not be a good idea, and Miss Fannie had frowned. But Mama? She would have straightened him out in her gentle, no-nonsense way.

And she probably would have been right, as she usually—

Wait. What was that smell?

He glanced around. The women surrounding him had started to back away. Far away.

"Jase, you need to change that diaper," one of them said.

No...

He girded up all his strength and prepared himself for a disaster.

The way opened for him to head into the building, and Pastor David must have caught sight of them—or smelled them, even from inside the church—because he burst out of the foyer's glass doors and strode toward Jase on the paved parking lot. His gait was steadier than it had been a year ago, but he still carried his cane, although it barely touched the ground with each step. A far cry from his previous Parkinson's shuffle that had contributed to a couple of bad falls before he'd started taking Rock Steady Boxing classes at Abe's gym last year.

"Everybody please give Pastor Jase some room. We'll answer your questions before the announcements," he said, putting all his authority into his voice and gesturing for them to make way. Then he stopped, made a face, and backed away. "My word, what is that noxious smell?"

Just as Jase met Pastor David at the canopy, a fire-red Jeep pulled up at the door. He peered in the driver's window. Sure enough, it was Mama. But why had she stopped here instead of the parking lot?

Then he noticed an elderly redhead in the front passenger seat, along with a pretty blonde in the back.

Mama had picked up Miss Fannie and Erin.

Apparently, Miss Fannie's light-headedness from this morning had subsided and she'd decided to come to church after all, so she must have called Mama to come and pick them up. Or she was merely powering through her discomfort, knowing Jase would need help. Either way, it was a nice surprise.

Or not. Because when Erin got out, looked Jase's way, and gave him a little smile and a wave, the questions started all over again—this time about her. But from a distance. By now, the church was probably empty, since it seemed every one of their sixty members was out here in the parking lot.

"Are you doing okay?" Erin called, her eyes twinkling as she took in the sight of Jase surrounded by women.

"Sure. Nothing wrong here."

Apparently, his sarcasm was lost on Erin, since she left him to fend for himself.

When he managed to make it to the door, Darnell held it open, his grin wide. "Hi, Bella," he said, puffing up a little and showing off his inside knowledge of the situation to the teens around him.

And it felt just right to Jase, since Darnell rarely experienced this kind of belonging. Bella had already begun to bless the people Jase loved.

Backing off, Darnell held his nose. "Whoo, she sure can make a stink!"

Yeah, well.

Jase hurried across the foyer to the men's room, mentally reviewing all his instructions on diaper changing. He pushed open the door. Wouldn't you know, the bathroom was packed with guys who'd had way too much coffee this morning.

The men bantering at the sinks all turned

toward him—or rather, toward the smell, probably—and stopped midsentence. Then a full three seconds of dead silence.

"Pastor Jase? What—" Rob Richards, head deacon, shook his head, his mouth open. "I don't... I don't know what to say."

"I'm just—" Could this possibly get more awkward? "I'm looking for a place to change her diaper."

"Dude, this ain't it." Piano player and Harley rider Zeke Holmes buried his nose and mouth in his elbow as he shouldered past Jase and out the door.

Jase glanced around the men's room, looking for a pull-down changing table—an item he wouldn't even have known existed if he hadn't cleaned the ladies' room during the janitor's vacation last month.

Not seeing one, he headed back out to the foyer and overheard Zeke talking to Pastor David. "You better get in the men's bathroom and get Pastor Jase under control. He needs some help."

Yes, he did. Because where could a man go to change a baby in this church? The nursery was stripped for new carpet and drywall. The kitchen? That seemed gross. First thing in the morning, he was going to order a changing table for the men's bathroom, if he had to pay for it himself.

Pastor David strode his way, coming to save him. Hallelujah.

"Where can I change her diaper?" Jase asked as soon as the pastor reached him. "I'm about ready to take her to my office and change her on top of my desk."

"Don't do that. It's right next to my office, and I don't want that stink in there." He peered inside the sanctuary. "Your mama just walked in. I'll get her."

"No!" When Pastor David spun his head around, eyes wide, Jase realized he'd shouted. "Sorry. But I have to do this myself. Bella is my responsibility, and I have to learn to take care of her."

His pastor let out a huge sigh. "Fine. But you'll have to do it on the changing table in the ladies' room."

Oh, no, he wasn't. "There's no way you're dragging me in there during church time."

"You don't have a choice." Pastor David gestured toward gray-haired Myra Cooper as she hobbled by with the aid of her walker. "Sister Myra, would you please check the ladies' room and see if anyone's in there? Pastor Jase needs to change this baby's diaper."

Sister Myra gave him a funny look but angled her walker in that direction. Moments later, she bellowed, "Y'all get out! Pastor Jase needs the bathroom!"

Jase's neck and face flamed, and he had to stand there while women and girls of all ages fled the bathroom, a touch of anxiety in the eyes of some. Were they afraid Jase would walk right in before they got out? Or were they afraid Sister Myra would bang into them with her walker if they didn't get out fast enough?

From the look of things, this could go either way.

"All clear, Sister Myra?" Pastor David called.

The elderly woman stretched her neck and peered inside. "Anybody in there?"

No one came out, so either the room was empty or whoever was in there was scared to come out.

"They gone." Sister Myra turned to them and started her trek to the sanctuary, muttering something about wet-behind-the-ears pastors and squalling babies.

As Jase waved his thanks, Pastor David corralled two fifth-grade girls coming in from outside. "Stand here by the door and make sure nobody goes in the bathroom until Pastor Jase comes out."

The girls' gazes flew from the pastor to Jase

to the still-crying baby, hands over their noses as they inched toward the ladies' room door.

"Okay, Jase, you can go on in." Pastor David made like he was going into the sanctuary.

Jase stopped him with a snort. "I'm not putting one foot in there unless you go with me."

The pastor sighed—again—and looked at his watch. "All right. Give me a moment."

Was this the way it was going to be for the next eighteen years? Well, obviously not the diaper part, but the part about Jase bumbling around, making a fool of himself while he tried to figure out how to take care of Bella. How did people do this, anyway? Rosemary and Abe always made parenting look so easy.

Then again, Rosemary and Georgia hadn't been around when Georgia was this age.

Next thing he knew, Pastor David's voice blasted through the speakers. Probably because Bella was crying so loudly, nobody would have heard his voice without the mic.

Well, that might be an exaggeration, but the tiny girl sure was making a great big noise.

"The service will start a few minutes late this morning. Zeke, please come to the piano and play a song or two while we wait."

As Pastor David came back up the aisle, Zeke sang the opening line to the old song "Change

My Heart, O God" and gave Jase a big grin and a thumbs-up.

Would this morning ever end?

Chapter Four

Ten minutes later, after one of the girls had run into the sanctuary to get Mama during what seemed like the fifteenth chorus of Zeke's so-funny song, Jase collapsed into the chair across from Pastor David's desk.

"I've never seen a mess like that in my life," Jase said, more exhausted than he'd ever felt after a weeklong youth camp.

"It was a bad one, that's for sure." His pastor took a long look at Bella, clean again, thanks to Mama and no thanks to Jase, and back in her car seat on the floor. "You're right. She looks just like Courtney."

"She's my cousin made over, all right." Amid yet another wave of grief over losing Courtney, Jase let his gaze wander over Bella's perfect features. "Hair, eyes, mouth—even the way she demands food from me."

"I'm glad you called me last night to let me know what's going on. This is big news for our congregation." He lowered his voice, gave Jase a sly grin. "Especially among the young women."

"Yes, they all seem to think I need a solution wife, and they're volunteering for the job."

Pastor David smirked a little. "I can think of worse problems."

Sure, except that, as soon as he'd agree to stand up at the altar while his "solution" walked down the aisle, she'd try to convince him to leave the ministry. Or she'd leave him at the altar. Or she'd marry him anyway and then demand he forsake his calling for her, leaving him wishing for an escape.

No, at the moment, Jase couldn't think of a worse problem.

"At any rate," the pastor said, "I'm sad to hear about Courtney. It must be hard to cope with her death, as close as you two were, while learning to care for a new baby."

Yes, but he'd found time for prayer and a few tears during the darkest hours of the night. "I think you were wise to suggest telling my story at the beginning of the service. That way, people can focus on the music and the sermon afterward, instead of thinking about Bella and me."

"Right." Pastor David looked at his watch and started for the door. "Time to start. Let's head to the platform, and you can introduce Bella to the congregation."

Jase unfastened the car seat's restraint and lifted Bella into his arms, leaving the seat behind. Between Mama, Miss Fannie and Erin, they wouldn't need it.

They started down the hallway that led to the baptistery at the back of the platform, bypassing the congregation for once instead of greeting them while walking down the aisle as they usually did. When they stepped out of the baptistery door, a hush fell on the room.

Last Sunday, when Jase stood at this podium to greet the congregation and read the announcements, he'd had no idea he'd have a baby with him today. Or that Courtney would be gone and his world would change forever.

Now, looking out at the people—his people—he realized everything hadn't changed, after all. Mama, Abe, Rosemary and Georgia sat as always in the second pew, stage left, with Miss Fannie and Miss Eugenia. Erin sat there today, too, already seeming like one of them.

Darnell and the rest of the youth group sat in their usual spot in the front two rows, stage right. Several other Rock Steady Boxing members and corner people were here, too, including Rosemary's father, Judge Burley Williams, and her mom, Miss Cozette. Rick and Erica Blaize—Darnell's foster parents—and their two primary-age kids. Abe's staff from the gym, Mackenzie Ward and Lauren Slater.

And the rest of the congregation, who had become like extended family.

Jase grabbed his headset, next to Pastor David's on top of the pulpit as always, then realized he couldn't put it on and hold Bella at the same time. So instead, he dropped it back on the pulpit, stepped down from the platform and carried Bella down the narrow middle aisle, showing her to one side and then the other.

"This is Bella May Armstrong. Her mama— my cousin Courtney—used her dying breath to instruct the doctors to give her to me. She is four days old, and tomorrow we meet with attorney Joseph Duncan to start adoption paperwork." Having reached the end of the aisle, he turned and started down a side aisle so the people on the ends could see her. "Everybody here probably knows about Miss Fannie's recent health challenges, and we've hired Erin Tucker to live at Rosewood with us for a few weeks until Miss Fannie is completely recovered. Erin is a nurse, and she's helping us take care of Bella, too. She's got her hands full, teaching me how to take care of such a little baby."

Jase could imagine how much all those female arms out there itched to hold Bella, so he breathed a quick prayer for tact and to speak the truth in love. "We want y'all to be involved in Bella's life. But because she's an orphan, we need to give her time to adjust and bond with us. So we're asking you to be patient as we limit the number of people who hold her. For now, that's just Miss Fannie, Erin and me. And my family, because I can't imagine trying to keep Mama from occasionally rocking Bella to sleep. We hope you understand."

He took the stairs to the platform again and, still without his mic, made the announcements loudly enough that even one-hundred-year-old Mr. Forbes seemed to hear. Then he stepped down, gave Bella to Mama, and sat with his family for the song service, something he hadn't done in years. It felt good to see Mama holding little Bella next to him.

An hour later, Pastor David closed the service, and this amazing group of people—his church family—crowded the aisle to welcome their smallest member into their church and lives.

Pastor David joined them, too, and held up

his hand for silence. "Let's pray for this newly created family."

As the pastor bowed his head, Jase scanned the sanctuary to check on the teens, as he always did whenever the adults' attention had shifted to prayer. He knew from experience that this was prime time for kids to get in trouble.

Sure enough, Darnell was slipping out the side door with Chance Boyer, a new kid who'd been getting detention for fighting and for smoking in school.

Jase hesitated, not wanting to jump to conclusions. But he'd been in the ministry long enough to know that, whenever he suspected a problem with one of the teens, he needed to check it out.

Even when it involved a kid who was trying as hard as Darnell was.

With everybody's eyes closed, Jase sneaked from his aisle seat and followed Darnell and Chance outside. He found them hanging around the front entrance, near Miss Eugenia's decorated golf cart, their backs to him and their voices low.

"What's up, men?" Jase called, maintaining a friendly tone as he strode closer.

Chance spun around, his face hard, as if he expected Jase to call him out. "We're not doing nothing."

A quick glance revealed no contraband, no reason to think they were getting into trouble. Darnell just stood there, hands in his pockets—nothing rebellious or unusual in his attitude. "That's good. But remember the rule—all the teens need to stay inside during the service."

"Looked to me like it was over," Chance said, his tone bordering on insolent. "Pastor David already dismissed everybody."

That much was true. "You're right. That's because we hadn't planned to pray for my family afterward. Still, let's go back inside and see if the prayer's over."

He clasped them both by the shoulder, giving them each a brotherly squeeze on the way to the side door. In the sanctuary again, he stopped them just inside the entrance, since the congregation still had their heads bowed in prayer.

Then he noticed Erin, her attention not on the prayer, but on him and the boys. Her brown eyes registered surprise. Then she looked over at Mama and Bella. She blinked a few times—fast—dropped her gaze and fiddled with her bulletin.

What was that all about?

Then it hit him. She must be as concerned for Darnell and Chance as Jase was. Because one look at the boys showed what was going on in their hearts. Darnell with his stooped posture and lowered gaze, and Chance, his chin jutted, eyes hard. Her compassion melted Jase a little, and for the first time since he met her—a day ago that seemed like a month, after all they'd been through together—he wished she'd stay.

Not for romantic reasons, of course. But, however it had happened, he'd grown comfortable with her presence, with her pretty eyes and her kind heart. Friendship, that's what it was. And now he sort of missed her calming smile.

Because she'd saved him. Maybe not physically, but without her, Jase didn't know how he would have coped these past twenty-four hours.

He ushered the boys to the row of chairs nearest the praying crowd. Then he walked right past the empty aisle seat to Mama's left and sat by Erin instead, knowing full well what it would look like to the congregation.

It would look like romance.

Stir up trouble.

Maybe even hurt some feelings.

He'd have to deal with that later, no matter how difficult. Because it wasn't every day that a brown-eyed beauty showed up on his doorstep to save him from disaster.

Erin was being foolish, reacting this way, and she knew it. But something about seeing Jase standing there with Darnell and another boy, leaving the baby behind, not being there for her during such a sacred and special time of prayer...

It had made her heart ache for little Bella. And reminded her too much of her father's belief that ministry comes before family. Even on the most important night of Erin's life.

Would Bella grow up as Erin had, feeling everyone in church was more important to her father than she was?

Then again, Jase had been a dad only one day, so he hadn't had time to realize he needed to pull back a bit from the ministry when his family needed him. Besides, she was leaving in two weeks. His child-rearing methods didn't involve Erin.

Except they did, because little motherless Bella had already stolen her heart.

Then she remembered last night, in the kitchen, when Jase had man-hugged Darnell and comforted him. What was it he'd said?

I know how it feels when your dad walks out.

Jase clearly knew what dysfunction looked like, felt like. So maybe today was a onetime event, and he'd raise Bella differently than Erin's dad had raised her.

If so, he'd sure have to clamp down on his overactive ministry drive. Because if Jase Armstrong was anything, he was passionate about his calling.

That afternoon, after eating way too many wedding leftovers served on Miss Fannie's favorite antique Spode dishes, Erin supervised as Jase fed and diapered Bella in the parlor-bedroom. Even in this short time, it seemed the baby had begun to bond with him, if the way she gazed at him was any indication. Now Bella rested in Miss Fannie's arms as she sat on her daybed, where she'd been much of the afternoon.

"Her eyes are getting heavy, Jase. Would you like to rock her to sleep here, and then put her in the cradle?" Miss Fannie's own eyes showed signs of fatigue after hosting a houseful of Jase's family, Pastor David and assorted other church members and teens for lunch. Although they didn't let her do any of the work. "That way, you won't have to carry her all the way up to your apartment."

Which probably meant Miss Fannie merely wanted the baby to stay with her. Erin turned away so the older lady couldn't see her grin. How sweet that the Lord had provided Bella with a grandmother figure.

Jase took the baby and sat in the rocker with Bella, but she fussed and squirmed. "I think she wants you, Miss Fannie."

The older woman leaned forward and peered at the baby. "Maybe she doesn't want to lie like that in your arms. Try holding her on your shoulder." She demonstrated, pretending to hold a baby in that position. "Like this."

Jase fumbled to maneuver her around, and Erin hurried to help. "If you lean back in the rocker when you change position, gravity will work with you and make it easier to keep a good hold on her."

"Right." Shifting as Erin suggested, he managed to get Bella on his shoulder. Soon she closed her big blue eyes in sleep, and Jase laid her in the cradle. "We're good for another two hours. I hope."

"Are you sure you can rest with her in here?" Erin asked Miss Fannie as she retrieved the old-fashioned manual blood pressure cuff, stethoscope and notebook from the armoire.

"I'm sure. The sound of a baby breathing relaxes me."

As Erin put the cuff on Miss Fannie's upper arm and the stethoscope tips in her own ears, Jase again settled into the rocker beside the cradle. "Fine with me. Erin, are you going to nap, too? It's our favorite Sunday afternoon activity. Even Darnell is crashed on a sofa in the upstairs center hall."

She pumped up the cuff and then in a few

moments, she let out the air. "I thought I might take Tasha for a walk around the estate, if you and Jase don't need me, Miss Fannie."

"Go whenever you want. We'll be fine." She leaned over, seeming almost to strain her eyes to see the numbers Erin wrote in her notebook. "Am I healthy?"

"Your vitals are good." She recorded the numbers and put away her equipment. "Your blood pressure is one twelve over sixty, the best it's been since you got home from the hospital, and your pulse is steady and strong."

Miss Fannie lay back on the daybed. "Good. I don't want anything to interfere with our evening. On Sunday nights, we make pizza and popcorn and play Hounds Head."

"Hounds Head? I've never heard of it. Is it a card game, like Sheepshead?"

Jase removed the dirty burping cloth he still had on his shoulder and dropped it into the wicker laundry basket at his side. "It's cards and much more."

How long had it been since Erin played a game with friends? Suddenly, the notion appealed to her more than thoughts of the Hamptons, Paris or even her dream: Osaka, Japan, where her father's parents had been missionaries.

Then she reined in that thought. Rosewood

had lots of guests coming and going, and Miss Fannie treated her like an equal. But the truth still remained: Erin was hired help. Jase probably didn't see her that way, since he was technically hired help himself, but an older lady like Miss Fannie might. Erin needed to remember that fact. "I think I'll take that walk."

Jase stood from the rocker. "Want me to come along and give you a tour? This estate's pretty amazing. We could take Sunny, too."

She should say no. She'd begun to admire Jase's kindness and love for everyone the Lord dropped into his life. Not to mention the way he tenderly cared for Bella. All the more reason to keep her distance from him as much as she could, given their situation. Since she was leaving in two weeks, and since Jase would always be a preacher, she couldn't let herself fall for him.

Doing so would only break her heart.

"Why don't you and Erin walk down to River House after you've seen the grounds?" Miss Fannie said as she pulled an afghan over her knees. "She could probably give you some decorating ideas."

"What's River House?" Erin said. "It sounds like an inn."

"Just a little place I'm trying to fix up as a

ministry venue for the youth. I doubt we'll have time today, but I'll show it to you soon."

From the look on Miss Fannie's face, she might have patted his cheek if she'd been close enough. "It's more than that. River House is Jase's vision for giving all Natchez's young people a place to belong, whether they go to River Church or not."

A place to belong…

Of course Jase would think of making the kids feel at home and loved. What if someone in her hometown had started a ministry like that? How much difference could it have made in her life—in her friends' lives? She pulled down the shade so Miss Fannie could rest without the sun in her eyes. "I'd like to see River House."

Erin glanced at the case clock—a quarter after two. A walk with Jase seemed worth the risk. Besides, the dogs needed the exercise, and so did she. "Can we take Tasha and Sunny to River House? Or is it too far?"

"Natchez is a small town," he said. "Nothing is very far from anything else."

Good. "I'll change and get Tasha's leash while you corral Sunny."

He turned to Miss Fannie. "I'll tell Darnell to come downstairs in case you want anything.

And I'll have my cell phone, so call me if you need me."

Erin went to her room next door and changed into pink athleisure pants, a long-sleeved white T-shirt, a zip-front gray sweatshirt and leopard sneakers. She pulled her hair into a high ponytail and headed back to the hall.

Jase had changed into black running pants and a gray Easily Distracted by Mustangs hoodie and looked as if he could run a 10-K as well as he could preach a wedding. Both dogs panted at his side, just outside her door, probably sensing their upcoming adventure. "Want to grab another glass of lemonade on the way out? There's a little left over from dinner."

She smiled at his old-fashioned habit of calling the noon meal "dinner." Or was it a Southern thing? "Are you kidding? That was the best lemonade I've ever had. You made it, right?"

"Sure. It's easy."

"Something was different about it. Do you share your recipes? I might try to make it sometime."

His lopsided grin tugged at her heart, and she looked away before it could pull her in. "Rosewood lemonade has two secret ingredients."

Erin grabbed Tasha's hot-pink leash from the round hall table and fastened it to her dog's collar, then ran her hand down the sweet little corgi's head and back. "I'm nearly useless in the kitchen, other than cleaning up, but I'd still like to know your secrets."

They started down the hall with both dogs and stopped at the kitchen. "All my secrets, or just my secret lemonade recipe?"

Standing at the kitchen counter, he suddenly seemed open, vulnerable. Less like the man with enough confidence to handle a wedding gone wrong and unruly teenagers.

Of course he had secrets. Everyone did. But did his involve heartache, like hers? Could they have anything to do with the fact that the Natchez Wedding Preacher, so handsome he'd outshine any groom, was single? And apparently not dating anyone either, since a girlfriend would surely be here helping him with the baby. The crowd of young women swarming him and Bella this morning also suggested he had no one special. If he did, they'd have known it and kept a respectable distance. Maybe. "Let's start with the recipe and move on from there."

Erin had no idea why she'd said that, since she had no right to ask him about his personal life. She never would, since she'd soon leave and never see him again. No more secrets, no more fancy lemonade—no more Jase. She needed to remember that.

He grabbed two insulated tumblers from a

kitchen cabinet as Erin crossed to the refrigerator and retrieved the pitcher of leftover lemonade. Then he added ice and poured. "If I spill the secret, you have to drink the whole glass."

"Deal."

"Okay, it's lavender and a pinch of salt."

"Salt? What?" She sipped a tiny amount, maybe a spoonful, but she still loved it. "This might be my favorite drink now. But I can't believe there's salt in here."

"It cuts the acid of the lemon. I also squeeze a couple of oranges into each batch."

Who knew you could glam up lemonade like that? "And the lavender?"

"The lavender part might not be completely reproducible, since I cut it fresh from a hundred-year-old bush in the herb garden. Young plants or a different variety might not produce the same result."

She twisted off her lid and peered into the tumbler. "I don't see any lavender leaves in here."

"I sugar the sprigs and then infuse them by pouring boiling water over them and letting them steep, like tea."

Suddenly, it seemed he was talking about more than lemonade—maybe about life. Relationships steeped in time and eventually strained of the dross, leaving behind a sweet love and belonging that nourished and refreshed. Bringing joy and even healing to those close to them.

And celebrating life. And love. And peaceful Sunday afternoons that brought perspective to a hectic week.

Wouldn't that be a perfect way to live?

And wouldn't Rosewood be the perfect place to live it?

The thought surprised her so much she had to make sure her jaw hadn't dropped. Having a home? Staying in one place longer than a few months? Running from a traditional lifestyle had been her escape since her double betrayal drove her from home.

But sometimes, in the darkest nights when sleep wouldn't come, she questioned her desire to run farther and farther from her childhood home in New York City, first to the Hamptons and then seeking adventure in faraway places. Would she never settle down? Would she merely drift from place to place for the rest of her life?

Most important at this moment, how did this sweet old home appeal to her more than the exciting life she'd lived the past three years? Maybe Rosewood's atmosphere made her wish for permanence, with its historic house and century-old herbs and slightly quirky owner who'd probably been alive during the Second World War.

Did it do the same for Jase? As he handed her the lid for her tumbler, she wondered for the first time at his choice of a home. Sure, he managed the estate, and he performed weddings for Miss Fannie's venue and looked after her. But that didn't mean he had to live here.

Maybe he felt the same way about it as she did. Or had one of his secrets driven him here? She took a good look at Jase as he sipped his lemonade, suddenly wishing she understood him better. Did he plan to live at Rosewood indefinitely? Maybe he was Miss Fannie's heir and would someday raise a family here.

She couldn't guess his feelings about this home or his reasons for immersing himself in it. She knew only that she loved this old estate. And at that moment, if Erin didn't know her wandering lifestyle kept her heart safe, she might never want to leave Rosewood.

Chapter Five

Jase had never been ashamed of his slightly sentimental side. If he had, he'd have been embarrassed to be known in Adams County, and beyond, as the Natchez Wedding Preacher. But at this moment, Erin's intense gaze and talk of secrets made him think she was trying to figure him out, wanting to understand why he kept his heart guarded. At least she couldn't see his battered heart and his abandoned desires for love and a family.

Maybe she'd guessed how deep his love ran for Miss Fannie, the woman who had given him back his sense of purpose—and his life—after his second breakup at the altar. That he hadn't come here just to serve her, but so she could serve him and help him recover. Of course, Erin couldn't know, because even as flighty as Miss Fannie could be, she'd never tell anyone what had happened that horrific day or how hopeless he'd felt. Even Jase didn't know how Miss Fannie had been able to pull him back from despair, when his mother, his brother and even Courtney couldn't.

Tasha let out a yip, and it sounded like she was telling Erin she was waiting, not so patiently, to go outside. Grateful for the distraction, Jase started for the back door, both dogs leading the way.

"Can we have this again with dinner?" Erin said then took a swig of her drink.

"Miss Fannie insists on lemonade all day long on Sundays." Jase took a sip from his tumbler and pointed toward the west. "Let's start your tour with the carriage house and garden cottages. It'll go faster, and it's almost time to start making pizza."

"And popcorn."

Erin's grin caught him off guard and somehow reminded him of yesterday, when they'd taken care of Miss Fannie at the chapel. When had a woman's innocent smile affected him this way? Had either of his fiancées had a smile that lit up their eyes? Dimples so cute he wanted to touch them? Or a silky-looking long ponytail that shone in the sunlight and made him think of a sandy beach on a warm spring day?

"Popcorn—yes. That's another of Miss Fannie's Sunday demands." As they passed the lion's head fountain, he scrambled for a conversation topic that would take his mind off how pretty Erin was. Then he remembered an unusual piece of jewelry she'd worn this morning. One that looked vaguely familiar. "I wanted to ask you…what kind of pin did you wear to church? I've seen one like it somewhere, but I can't remember where."

"My nurse's pin. Your mom probably wears one. Each nursing school has its own pin, but some of them look a lot alike."

That had to be it. But Mama didn't wear hers unless she was working… Oh. Sure, Erin had been on duty this morning, watching out for her patient. And keeping an eye on Bella during the service as well.

"I guess I put it on out of habit," she said as they reached the carriage house. Tasha pulled on the leash, wanting to head toward the lake behind them. Erin guided her back to the trail. "Maybe I should ask Miss Fannie if she wants me to wear it, because if she doesn't care, I'd rather not."

"Aren't all nurses proud of their pins?"

"Yes, they're special. To most of us, the pinning ceremony is more important than graduation." Erin swallowed, something like a broken dream filling her eyes. "But this one brings back memories. Bad memories."

Jase stopped and brought Sunny in to heel. "What kind?"

She blinked—hard—a few times. "The kind that reminds you how unimportant you are to people who should value you and be there for you. Especially on the most important night of your life."

"You mean someone should have shown up at the ceremony but didn't?"

"Not one person. Two. My father and my former fiancé." Erin rambled over to a camellia bush near the carriage house, plucked an early white blossom and held it to her nose.

He knew from experience how deceptive those delicate white blossoms were. The first flowers to bloom in the new year, they held no scent. How many times had he sensed a guest's disappointment as she drew in a breath of anticipation, but no sweet scent wafted toward her?

"Erin, I'm sorry. Your father—was he an absentee parent?" His throat suddenly dry, Jase raised his lemonade tumbler to his mouth. *Lord, please don't let this be another story of a deadbeat dad who spent the evening with his drink instead of his daughter.*

"Yes, he was absent." Her voice was little more than a whisper, the corners of her eyes moist. She dropped the flower in the grass and turned her attention to Jase. "He was a preacher."

A chill went through Jase like the February riverbank wind. "Maybe he had a good reason for missing your ceremony…" Even as he said it, he had a feeling it wasn't true.

"He thought he did. But it happened all the time. He was always somewhere else, with someone else, when I needed him. This time, he took my fiancé with him to the hospital when a boy in the youth group had been in an accident. Neither of the men in my life showed up for me that day. So Mom was the only one who came up onto the platform with me when they called my name. She gave me my rose and fastened my pin to one side of my collar and Grandma Tucker's nursing pin on the other side. Dad was supposed to do that."

Wow, this sounded a lot like a news story he'd read during his own darkest hours—a pastor's daughter breaking her engagement to a hotshot quarterback who'd openly spoken about his faith in Jesus. In fact, if the names had been the same, he'd have thought Erin had been the girl in the press release that night. He swiveled to see her profile, the one that had flashed on every screen on the continent, and imagined her with darker short, curly hair.

Come to think of it, that girl was from New York. And wasn't her last name Tucker?

It sounded right, but that woman's name wasn't Erin…

To hide his confusion, he took another long drink of lemonade. This couldn't be a coincidence. Even though the first names didn't match, this had to be the story he'd seen plastered all over social media and the news outlets back then. Jase stopped midgulp as he realized who Erin really was. At least, who he thought she was. "Erin," he choked out, "is your father Nick Tucker? The pastor at that big Times Square church?"

She said nothing, just nodded. But he could sense her pain, even in the silent gesture.

"So your fiancé was superstar quarterback Calum King."

Erin's silence grew almost painful. The song of a mockingbird reached them from the top of the giant oak towering over the cottages, reminding him, as always, that Rosewood was a place to heal. To grow. Maybe even to thrive one day. That's what happened to its owner after the tragedy that took her husband decades too soon.

And it's what had happened to Jase.

For a moment, he wished he could impart to Erin some of the healing he'd found here. But healing would take far longer than the short time she'd have at Rosewood.

"After Calum made his faith public, my dad invited him to speak at a big youth rally at our church. For some reason, he and Dad hit it off, and my father started inviting him to help with different ministry events. Then Calum decided he wanted to get into the ministry, using his fame to spread the gospel. So Dad started discipling him, taking him along to visit the sick and help guys who were getting out of jail, stuff like that. But he did that every single time he was in town. I think Calum enjoyed being with my dad more than me." She turned her gaze toward the lake. "Since you're a youth pastor, I'm guessing you read all about our breakup. Not that we were that big of a deal in reality. But all the gossip magazines and blogs wanted the story. Calum talked to them all."

"But you didn't. At least, not much," he said, feeling an irrational knot of guilt for knowing the details of her heartbreak.

"No, in my press release, all I said was that he'd stood me up for the last time. That made me the girl who dumped superstar quarterback Calum King. What I didn't tell the media was that standing me up had become Calum's habit, and it was always with my dad. Somebody needed prayer, or somebody needed their rent paid, or somebody was in the hospital." She took a sip of her drink, but her eyes were so filled with sadness, Jase wasn't sure she tasted it.

"I followed your story closely, because of what happened in my life that same week. I read every interview I could find, but all I remember you saying was that your dad was supposed to give you his mother's pin, and how both he and Calum stood you up. I thought there was more to it." Everything she said sounded right, except the name. Jase hesitated, choosing his words carefully. "But I thought that girl's name was Anna Tucker."

"My name is Erin Julianna Tucker, but I used to go by Anna. After the breakup, I stopped using my nickname because I was tired of being known as that girl. You can't imagine the nasty comments I got all over social media. Or maybe you saw them. It seemed as if every girl in America was in love with him and hated me."

And she didn't have any social media accounts anymore, either, as Jase had discovered during her hiring process. He always checked out applicants' social media before offering a job, but with Erin, he'd not only found nothing questionable, but he'd found nothing at all.

"I never want to be neglected that way

again," she said. "That's why I'll never fall in love with a preacher."

If she'd said the words with the slightest trace of bitterness, they would've been easier to hear. But her tone was as gentle as if she were talking to Bella. Gentle, but pain filled. It tore out a piece of what was left of his heart, and it made him want to drive to Times Square and have a heart-to-heart with Reverend Tucker and tell him how a minister should treat his daughter.

Except Jase had done the same thing this morning, although on a smaller scale.

But what was he supposed to do, when Darnell and Chance had clearly violated youth group rules and could have been getting into trouble? He didn't think Darnell would have intentionally done anything wrong out there, but Chance was another story.

And yet he'd left the room while the church prayed for his daughter.

He'd have to think about this later, pray about it. Make every effort to avoid hurting Bella the way Reverend Tucker had hurt Erin.

Sunny must have sensed a rabbit or a squirrel nearby, because she pulled hard on the leash. Jase called her to heel and glanced at the time on his phone. He gestured toward the two cottages near the house. "It's getting too late to go to River House. Want to sit on one of the cottage porches for a few minutes, then go inside?"

They left the stable area without even stepping into the reception venue. Closer to the big house, they stopped when they reached the two empty cottages that sat waiting for repairs and updating.

On the porch of the cottage nearest the big house, the dogs lay on the wooden floor while Jase and Erin each took a white rocker. "You said something happened to you during the week of my pinning. I hope it was a happy event," she said, gazing out toward the gardens with their early camellias and purple irises.

He couldn't hold back the bark of a mirthless laugh that escaped him like cannon fire.

Where had that staccato bite of sarcasm come from? Immediately, he repented of such ingratitude, vowing not to let it happen again. Not after the way the Lord had helped him through the pain of that day. "No, it was not a happy event."

Although he didn't look at her—couldn't look at her after his outburst—he could feel her gaze upon him. He guessed that her eyes were bulged in surprise. "I'm sorry about reacting that way. I still have some big issues here."

"Do you want to tell me?"

Her soft voice, seasoned with kindness,

tempted him to spill everything. Of course, he couldn't. But it might make him feel a little better if he told her about that day, especially after she'd admitted her struggles.

"I know when you broke your engagement," he said, "because mine ended the same day." One of them, anyway.

Erin reached down, picked up Tasha and snuggled her on her lap. The dog's big ears stood straight up, looking a little comical, but Jase had no room in his heart for laughter now. Even though it had been three years since Kayla, his first fiancée, had called it quits, and a year since Sydney had done the same thing.

"It happened right over there." Both times. Jase pointed toward the chapel at the other end of the lawn.

Erin's eyes went huge, and she leaned forward in her rocker, as if she could see Kayla and Sydney standing there if she tried a little harder. "She came out here and broke up with you on Rosewood's lawn?"

"Kayla came out here, all right. In a white dress and veil."

He could tell the moment she got it.

"Jase, no," she said, a little moan in her words. "At the altar?"

At first, all he could do was nod, thinking of standing at the same altar almost every week-end since then, usually marrying strangers but occasionally a pair of locals. It sometimes seemed as if he spent his life waiting for the next time somebody got dumped at the pretty little chapel. "Just like yesterday. She said she was sorry, shed a few tears and was gone."

"With no explanation?"

Oh, she had explained, all right. "She didn't want to be a minister's wife."

"Didn't she know that ahead of time?"

"She knew, but she thought she could change me. Talk me into forsaking my calling and leading a 'normal' life." And the next summer, she'd married a local high school teacher, who started coming to River Church with her.

That had been fun.

The next time was worse. Especially after the guests had gone home and the place was cleaned up, and Jase sat alone in the house he and Sydney had bought together.

Yeah, that night had gotten bad.

"I think that's the saddest story I've ever heard," she murmured, so low he almost missed it.

"Maybe, but you don't walk away from a calling from God, no matter what you have to do or what you have to give up. Don't worry about me, though. I'm not falling in love again, unless it's with a woman who's called to be a pastor's wife." Probably not even then.

"Is that a thing? A calling to be a pastor's wife? I never heard my mom say she had a calling."

He shrugged, gazing off toward the herb gardens, where their tame ducks waddled toward them on the brick walk. "All I know is Pastor David's late wife was called. She was awesome, always having people in her home, an older woman teaching the younger women, like the Bible says. And she could flat-out play the keys right off the piano."

As if he'd ever find a woman like that. If he did, both he and the woman would probably be so old, she'd already be teaching the women Erin's age. He puffed out a breath of discouragement, wishing he could forget his morbid thought but not quite able to let it go.

"I can't play the piano, but I can play the bassoon."

What? Was she kidding? He turned to catch her eyes twinkling and her fingers pressed against the smile they couldn't quite cover.

And then he got it.

Erin had sensed his mind was heading toward a dark place, and she'd used her silly little comment to try to pull him back.

Just the thought of it made him smile. "Bassoon, huh? Last time I heard one of those was at the junior high Christmas recital, blasting like a moose."

"I can play it loud, too. So let me know when you're ready to add the bassoon to your worship service."

Before he could think of a reply, he caught a glimpse of somebody riding a bike up the service drive and then up the sidewalk that led to the back gallery.

Chance Boyer.

"Let's go back," he said, lowering his voice. "I think that was Chance, sneaking in rather than using the drive. We might have trouble."

Jase stood and started toward the house with Sunny, quickly breaking into a run. He could hear Erin following close behind, little Tasha apparently keeping up on her three short legs.

"What's going on?" she whispered as they crossed the brick courtyard and headed toward the gallery.

"It might be a repeat of this morning, whatever that was. Or it might be nothing." They reached the back door, and he held it open for her and the dogs. "But one thing I've learned in my four years of youth ministry—if things smell fishy, they probably are."

And right now, the situation with Chance smelled like a forty-pound Mississippi River flathead catfish.

When Erin came to Rosewood to be a nurse to Miss Fannie and an infant-care instructor to Jase, she hadn't realized she was also signing up as pinch-hitter youth group teacher. But now, with Jase in the closed-door kitchen with Darnell and Chance, here she was, helping Miss Fannie with her therapy exercises while trying to formulate a teaching for the six girls who sat on the back gallery. If they were still there by the time Erin was ready, and if they weren't getting into trouble, too, the kind Jase was dealing with before making pizza with the boys. And if they wanted to hear anything Erin had to say.

But Jase thought teen girls needed to hear a woman teach from time to time. And with his smooth, deep Southern drawl, he'd convinced her to try.

Now she was sure that was a mistake.

"Miss Fannie, when Jase asked me to teach the girls tonight, I tried to say no. I have no idea how to reach those girls. I've never taught youth group before, except in high school when my dad made me teach the junior high kids a couple of times. I was terrible at it. I'm not qualified."

"Jase thinks you are," Miss Fannie said.

"That's just because I'm a pastor's kid." She looked at the clock. "Even if I was qualified, he wants me to teach in ten minutes. That's not enough time to put together a lesson."

"Eight, nine, ten." Her patient obediently counted her leg lifts as she mirrored Erin's actions. They sat facing each other on the dining room chairs Erin had brought into the parlor-bedroom for the exercises the physical therapist had given her at this afternoon's visit. "You haven't heard Jase preach," Miss Fannie said, sounding a little winded with her effort. "He never writes an outline or prepares a sermon with an introduction, three points and a conclusion, like he says they taught him in Bible college. He doesn't expect you to, either."

Erin demonstrated the next exercise—ankle rotations. They started together, Miss Fannie counting.

"What does he do?"

"Five, six… He says he studies the Word and learns it for himself…seven, eight…and then he teaches from what he's absorbed into his life. Nine, ten."

"Now go the other way with both ankles."

"One, two…"

"That's fine for him. I don't know how to do that."

"Then just think of some way the Lord has helped you or how the Bible has spoken to you, and tell them about it. Seven, eight, nine, ten."

Bella started making little squeaking sounds from her cradle, and Erin was glad for the distraction. She leaned over and picked her up, breathed in her sweet newborn scent. "Poor, sweet baby. What's the matter?"

Erin held her closer and cradled her head. Could a child this young be confused, wondering where her mother was? Might Bella be lonesome, frightened without hearing Courtney's voice, her heartbeat?

Mom used to say she sang "All Through the Night" to Erin when she was fussy. She hummed a few bars of the ancient song, and the baby quieted.

Footsteps sounded through the hall, and then Jase stood at the door. "I thought I heard her making noise. Okay for me to come in?"

"Whenever the door is open, come in," Miss Fannie said. "So should everyone else. In fact, I want y'all in here, keeping me company, every chance you get. Since the parlor and library are our bedrooms now, we're running out of places to sit together."

"We could make the hall into more of a sitting area." Erin glanced out the door. "Maybe push the round center table against the wall and take some chairs out of our rooms and set them up in the hall."

Miss Fannie hesitated as she peered out into the hall. "We've never used the downstairs hall as a sitting room as we have upstairs."

"Maybe it's time to make a new tradition," Jase said.

"I don't know…it's just not done that way."

"We've never let that stop us before. Besides, with all the extra furniture in here, there's not room to play Hounds Head." He gestured around the room. "We need four indoor playing areas besides the dartboard. So unless we move the game into the hall, I don't think we can play."

Dartboard? Erin glanced at the baby in her lap. "Magnetic darts, I hope. Otherwise, Bella can't be there."

"Magnetic is always best with junior high kids," Jase said as his daughter batted her fists in the air, eyes tightly closed and lips parted in a low howl. He grasped one hand and gave it a little kiss. "Maybe she's hungry. I think I can manage her bottle so you can finish your exercises."

"We're done," Erin said, handing him the baby so she could spot Miss Fannie while she got out of her chair. The aromas of spices and yeast mingled with Jase's usual scent of sandalwood and cardamom and lingered around him. He must have been cooking and dealing with Darnell and Chance at the same time. She drew another breath of the appealing mixture of fragrances that made her both hungry and wary. No matter how good this man smelled, she still had to distance herself. "How's it going with the boys?"

"I made them tell me what the deal was at church this morning," he said, his voice lowered. "All Darnell would say was that he followed Chance outside to keep him out of trouble. Chance won't talk, so I don't know what he was up to. But he wants to see Bella."

What? Chance was interested in a baby? She hadn't expected that.

Over the sound of Bella's cries, ever increasing in pitch and volume, she heard laughter from the direction of the kitchen—wholesome adolescent-boy laughter, not the kind you hear when boys are being ornery.

"Let's take her in the kitchen," Jase said, "and one of us can feed her while the other cooks."

Erin settled Miss Fannie on her daybed and covered her knees with a nearby, old-fashioned quilted lap robe, then set her glass of water on the table next to her, along with her phone and an antique silver bell she could ring if she needed Erin.

"That means I'll take baby duty. I promise you—putting me to work in a kitchen is a big mistake."

But an even bigger mistake would be having Erin teach the girls a Bible lesson. When they stepped into the hall, Erin touched his arm and gestured for him to come with her to the corner. "I wish I could help with the girls, but I just can't," she whispered. "I know everybody thinks a pastor's daughter should be able to do ministry. But I was never interested in that, so I didn't learn." She hesitated, not wanting to be overly dramatic, but needing him to know how badly this would turn out. "It would be a disaster."

"Don't worry," he said. "Maybe we'll skip Bible study tonight and move straight to the games after supper. Sort of a night off for our first Sunday with Bella."

Yes. Sweet relief. On impulse, she threw one arm around his waist and squeezed a little, being mindful of the baby. "Thank you!"

Stepping back, she dropped her gaze, her face hot.

Had she just hugged him? What was she thinking? And the look on his face—was it panic? She wasn't sure what it meant, but she was certain he wasn't happy about her friendly embrace.

"Sorry. I—I was so relieved, I just…forget it, okay?" Oh, she was making things worse. Even though she looked away, she couldn't escape the image of his expression. If she was brave enough to face him right now, what would she see? Fear? A frown?

Did she even want to know?

Not giving him a chance to respond, she hurried toward the kitchen as Bella's cries grew more demanding. Jase followed at a slower pace and caught up with her after she'd entered the kitchen, where Darnell and Chance stood over six giant pizzas, sprinkling a ridiculously large amount of cheese on the last two.

"All done," Darnell said as he stepped to the sink and washed his hands. "Both ovens are preheated and ready to go."

Chance, on the other hand, gazed at Bella. For the first time, Erin noticed his eyes. As he watched the baby, their deep brown depths reflected pain of some sort, something raw and unresolved. "Is she okay?"

"Other than hunger, she's fine." Erin's heart melted a little at Chance's concern—deep concern, if his slightly wavering voice meant anything. He probably hadn't been around babies much and didn't realize they all cried like this when they were hungry. She smiled and almost reached out to touch his arm in reassurance but remembered her innocent hug in the hallway and decided against it. No need to make the same mistake twice in ten minutes.

Chance took a step toward Jase and the baby, then stopped and turned back to the counter.

"Pizzas look great. Just right. Load 'em up, men." Jase raised his voice over the sound of Bella's cries. "Let's bake the first four. You used the convection oven setting, right?"

Darnell gave a fist pump and a grunt as he opened the door of the oven nearest him, slid in two pizzas and eased shut the door as if he'd been doing this forever. Chance put two more in the other oven.

"Looks like the boys have it under control," Erin said, holding out her arms for Bella. "Want me to take her so you can practice making the bottle?"

"More practice won't hurt." Jase transferred Bella into her care without making eye contact.

Wow, he sure must not have wanted that hug. That was okay with her, but she wouldn't make the same mistake again.

As she shifted Bella in her arms, swaying a

little to try to calm her, Chance inched up to her. He held out his index finger. "Can I touch her?"

Erin glanced at Jase, who had begun heating water for her milk. Of course, it was his decision.

He set down the measuring cup he'd taken from the cabinet. For just an instant, his face registered surprise, but he recovered before Chance followed Erin's gaze and turned to look at him.

"Sure you can, buddy."

The caring in Jase's warm smile seemed to spread over Chance like a blanket, and a tiny fraction of the chill melted from his demeanor. He brushed his finger over the back of the baby's little hand, swallowed hard and turned away, fast.

What had Erin just seen? This hadn't been mere curiosity or entertainment. Something about Bella had touched the boy. Suddenly she wanted to know why. Chance needed healing of some sort, and it seemed this baby girl might eventually help to bring it.

Chapter Six

As hard as he tried, Jase couldn't erase the memory of Erin's nanosecond hug from his mind. He also couldn't believe how such a spontaneous, so-quick-it-didn't-even-count gesture could erase all other thoughts from his mind. So much so that he'd forgotten all about the pizzas and had left them in the oven too long while the boys rearranged a few pieces of furniture in Miss Fannie's room to suit her better.

Why hadn't he smelled them? And when was the last time he'd burned food, especially pizza?

He'd hidden in the kitchen long enough with the boys. "Go ahead and put the other two in the oven, then bring these in the dining room. I'm just glad they didn't burn too badly." He'd make sure Miss Fannie got her meal from the last ones.

He grabbed another pitcher of lemonade from the refrigerator and carried it to the big formal dining room, where the youth always ate on Sunday nights. Apparently, Erin hadn't had any more success at getting a burp from Bella than Jase had, since the baby wasn't in the room with her as they'd planned. Miss Fannie must have been giving Bella her expert touch in the smaller family dining room. Now Erin sat at the table, surrounded by six junior high youth group girls who chattered about Bella and babies in general.

"I get to start babysitting as soon as I turn thirteen," Kiara Robinson said, glancing at Jase and grinning.

"Oh, yeah?" Jase said, tugging her braid as he passed behind her. "And give up your other job? The one where you have the greatest boss in the world?"

"You already have a job, Kiara?" Erin asked as he took the only available chair—the one across from her—and tried to avoid looking into her beautiful brown eyes.

She'd changed into a flowy-sleeved blue dress with a flower print, her hair falling down her back, and looked as pretty as she had in her bridesmaid attire. When she smiled at him, lighting those lovely eyes, he gave up his unrealistic goal of averting his gaze.

"My mamaw is the housekeeper here at Rosewood, and I help," Kiara said. "She pays me five dollars an hour and says I deserve ten."

"And your mamaw is your great boss?"

"Nope. It's me," Jase said.

After the girls' giggles died down, Kiara turned to Erin, her brown eyes big and pleading. "Can you teach us how to take care of a baby, Miss Erin?"

She laughed. "I wasn't able to get Bella to burp, so I might not be the best teacher. But one technique won't necessarily always work two days in a row. It doesn't work for every baby, either. So when you take care of a baby, think and use common sense. And listen to people who have experience caring for infants. Beyond that, all you need to do is love the baby. If you do, everything else will fall in line."

"I'm not sure how that works. Pastor David says if you walk in love, things work out." Kiara picked up her glass, made little designs in the condensation. "I love my mom, but she took off with a truck driver and left me with Mamaw. Loving Mama didn't make her stay or come back. And I'd love my dad if I knew him."

Wow, Jase had never heard Kiara open up like that. At least, not to him. Maybe he should leave the room so he wouldn't somehow mess this up. Before he could decide, Erin slipped her arm around Kiara, and he couldn't look away.

"Sweetheart, loving people doesn't make them do what we want them to do, and it doesn't force them to make the right decisions," she said. "Loving people means we forgive them, pray for them and treat them the way the Bible says. And that we trust the Lord to take care of our hearts when people we love hurt us."

"But if we forgive them, they get away with hurting us." Dark-haired Ashley Ward sat on Erin's other side. Considering her mom's recent shoplifting arrest, Ashley had a legitimate reason to want an answer.

"No, it doesn't work that way." Now Erin had her arms around both girls. "Yes, we have to forgive people, but each person has to ask God for forgiveness of their own sins. He doesn't automatically forgive them when you do. But He will continue to prick their hearts and encourage them to change and stop hurting you. Christianity is a life of change, you know."

Wow. And Erin thought she didn't have what it took to teach these sweet girls.

Darnell and Chance came in, each carrying a pizza. When they'd set them on the giant boards they used for trivets, Jase stood and tapped his glass with his fork, amid a loud cry from Bella in the next room. "My family's not here yet. But at Rosewood, we go ahead and start while the pizza's hot. Y'all bow your heads."

Jase had no more than finished his prayer when a bell tinkled from the direction of the smaller family dining room.

Erin jumped up and started for the hall. "Please don't wait for me. I'll be back after I take care of Miss Fannie."

As the kids dived into the pizza, a text message notification pinged from Jase's phone. It sat among the kids' phones on the antique walnut buffet against the wall, where he always insisted the young people keep them, notifications and ringers off, until they left for home. He glanced in that direction. It could be one of the kids' parents or caregivers, since they all knew Jase kept his phone on, in case they needed to get ahold of their child. Still, he waited until everybody was served pizza and lemonade before he retrieved his phone, trying to lead by example and show the kids that face-to-face relationships came before devices.

As he grabbed his phone, Erin returned, a pink burp cloth on her shoulder, the baby's cries growing louder. "Miss Fannie can't get Bella to burp. I tried again, too, but I couldn't do any better. I was hoping Rosemary would be here to help."

"Is Abe's truck in the driveway, Darnell?"

Jase asked, grabbing his phone to check the time. Six forty-five. They were never this late.

Darnell scooted back his chair, giant-stepped to the window and pulled back the curtain. "Not yet."

Jase remembered the text message and checked it.

Abe. Running late. Bandit had an accident on the rug.

Georgia's puppy.

Jase texted back a thumbs-up icon and slid his phone back onto the buffet. "What can we do to make her burp? She won't be comfortable until she does, right?"

"Let me try," Chance said, standing. "I know how."

"You do?" Jase asked.

"I'll show you."

This made no sense at all. Chance and his mom had lived in Natchez for only a month or so, but Jase had been to their apartment twice and hadn't seen a crib or toys or anything that suggested a baby lived there. Could he or she be living with Chance's dad?

Jase glanced at Erin, who merely shrugged. A gesture he took to mean that he was Bella's father, so he had to decide whether to let a teenage boy take his tiny daughter in his big, slightly grubby hands and try to coax a burp from her.

A little advice here, please, Lord...

Receiving no clear direction, he relied on the principles he'd always stuck to in the ministry: disciple believers by sharing, teaching and living his own faith, then trust the kids.

He never dreamed how much faith it would take to trust his Bella to one of his youth.

"Let's go." He pointed at Chance and gestured toward the door, then gave the rest of the kids a mock scowl. "I don't want to see pizza on the walls, ceiling or curtains when I get back."

Moments later, inside the small dining room, Chance sat in one of the fancy cherry chairs and gently took the baby from Miss Fannie, looking as comfortable as if he'd done it a hundred times. He set Bella on his lap, leaned her forward and supported her head by placing his forefinger and thumb under her jawbone. He rubbed up and down her back and made little baby-talk noises to her.

Bella's eyes looked more alert than Jase had ever seen them. It might have been his imagination, but she seemed to enjoy Chance's ministrations. And she rewarded him with a ladylike little burp. He gave Bella back to Miss Fannie.

Grinning, Erin whipped the burp cloth from her shoulder and swatted Chance with it. "How did you do that? Miss Fannie and I spent half an hour burping her the same way, and every other way we could think of. But you just walk in and get her to cooperate in less than thirty seconds."

Chance gave Erin one of the few smiles Jase had ever seen on his face. The boy puffed up at Erin's words, at her animated face and voice. Wow, she seemed to know exactly how to fill a teenage boy with confidence. And pride. The good kind of pride in a job well done.

"You're going to have to move in here with us and be the baby whisperer," she said, ruffling his hair like a big sister.

The glow in Chance's dark eyes shouted that Erin had won him over. A feat Jase had yet to accomplish. Chance might be the baby whisperer, but Erin was, without a doubt, the rowdy, cigarette-smoking, trouble-causing, kinda-smelly teenage-boy whisperer. And at this moment, she just about took Jase's breath away.

"Where did you learn to do that, Chance?" Miss Fannie gazed down at Bella, a little note of longing in her voice. It was almost as if she was thinking of all the babies she'd wanted to have and care for—to feed and burp—but who'd never made an appearance. "Do you have a baby brother or sister?"

Just like that, Chance turned back into the

sullen, rebellious kid with darkness in his eyes and hardness in his face. "Nope," he said, his tone harsh. He turned and dashed out to the hall, and within seconds, the back door slammed.

Miss Fannie's eyes grew large, her mouth slightly agape. "What—what did I say wrong?"

"Nothing. Something's going on with him, and he's hurting terribly," Erin said as Jase took off after Chance. He raced across the brick courtyard and reached the service drive in time to see the boy pedal to the bottom of the hill and onto the road to town.

Jase started toward the house again, and Erin met him in the courtyard. "Where's Chance?" she asked, glancing around in the dusk. The joy gone from her face, she fixed her gaze on the service drive, but the boy was gone.

"He took off. But don't let that discourage you. Chance took some big steps tonight, especially when he responded to you. I don't know how you did it, but you opened his heart." He laid his hand on her shoulder for a mere moment. "He'll be back."

If they'd been keeping score tonight, it would be Nurse Erin two, Pastor Jase zero. Because, no matter how he looked at it, she'd been the one touching these kids' hearts.

In fact, she'd done more for the youth tonight

than either of Jase's former fiancées had the entire time they'd dated.

He took a good look at Erin, her gaze flitting around the grounds as if she was still looking for Chance, and a new thought hit him. What if Erin had a calling on her life? He'd seen it before and knew what it looked like. Being called himself, he could see the signs. But, of course, signs didn't mean the calling was real. That took time and discernment.

The bad thing was, even if she was called, she didn't want to answer. And as far as Jase knew, the Lord didn't force people to serve Him in this way. If Erin ever did submit to a call, it wouldn't be here and now. She was far too hurt by the past and might need years to work through it.

For the first time, Jase wished Erin would stay at Rosewood a little longer.

Hvar, Copacabana, Maui—none of the glamorous places where Erin had accompanied her clients could compare to Rosewood tonight. This home, while spectacular in architecture, design and decor, held a warmth she'd never experienced in Croatia, Brazil or Hawaii.

And there'd never been a child's laughter or a newborn's sweet little gurgles or teenagers playing a silly game with a sillier name. Or an elderly, wise lady who knew more about giving than anyone Erin had ever met. Or girls with big eyes and bigger problems, who seemed to accept and love her on sight, probably because she was with Jase, whom they loved.

Well, not *with* him. Just working with him.

"Let's go, Miss Erin!" Kiara tugged on Erin's hand, pulling her toward station one in the game.

Kiara had snatched up Erin as her partner as soon as Jase announced game time, and Erin had agreed just as quickly. "We have five minutes at each game station to get as many points as we can," Kiara told her. "Let's try to get the card game first. It's my favorite."

The girl pulled Erin to the round table in the middle of the hall, where four decks of Dutch Blitz cards waited. Erin chose the stack with a picture of a red buggy on the back, and Kiara picked the yellow wooden bucket. The front of the cards had a picture of Dutch girls or boys, along with a number. As soon as Miss Fannie said go, their hands flew as they had five minutes to turn over cards and make stacks of ten, in numerical order, of the same color.

"Two-minute warning!" Miss Fannie cried into an old megaphone, the baby somehow sleeping in the cradle beside her.

"Faster, Miss Erin!" Kiara screamed.

Amid the din of the teams of teens, adults and little Georgia competing in seven different games, Erin kept her focus on flipping the cards and slapping them on the right stacks.

"Stop!" Miss Fannie's voice blasted from the megaphone. "Each team count your points and enter them on the whiteboard."

As team captains moved to the board and picked up markers, Miss Fannie motioned Erin and Rosemary to her side. "Are you sure all this noise is okay for the baby? The kids are loud, and the dogs are riled up, too. Georgia's Bandit is louder than anybody, including the boys."

Erin looked at Rosemary, remembering what she'd been taught in pediatrics class but deferring to Rosemary's experience as a mother.

"I think it's fine," she said, Georgia clinging to her hand as her partner. "If she was the youngest child in a large family, there'd be plenty of noise in the house every evening."

"I agree," Erin said, turning to the cradle. "If the noise scared her, she'd cry."

"Then that settles it." Miss Fannie raised her megaphone to her mouth. "Teams, move to the next station."

Kiara skipped up to Erin. "We got fifty-six points. You're awesome at Dutch Blitz!"

"I used to play it with my mom when I was your age."

They moved to game station two: badminton on the back lawn, where they hit as many birdies in a row as they could under the floodlights while Darnell and Ashley threw horseshoes. When they'd also finished Jenga and Yahtzee, Miss Fannie called for a halftime break.

She motioned for Erin. "Your phone has rung three times since we started," she said. "At least, it sounded as if it came from your room. I called a time-out so you could check it."

When she reached her phone, Danielle's name popped up, showing that Erin had missed her video call. Good. Maybe tonight Danielle would explain why she'd decided to leave Robert at the altar. Erin hit Dial and prayed for the right words.

"Where are you? What's that noise?" Danielle said with a beach background behind her. Her hair pulled back in a beyond-messy bun and wearing no makeup, she looked as if she hadn't slept since the wedding fiasco.

"It's a bunch of teens, a few adults, a four-year-old, a newborn baby and three dogs having church."

"O—kay."

Erin stepped out the front door and sat on a rocker on the porch—the gallery, as Jase and Miss Fannie called it. "I have a temporary job here in Natchez," she said, hesitating to tell

Danielle exactly where that job was. "I'm taking care of a sweet elderly lady who lives in a fabulous home."

"You had that when you worked for Mrs. Fairchild. But judging from your tone, you're more satisfied here than you were in Paris. What's up with that?"

Her tone? Sure, she'd loved Miss Fannie instantly, and Rosewood was amazing, but satisfaction? "It's nothing like that. I like it here, but it's just for two weeks."

Danielle went silent for a moment. "Be careful. Don't get used to a domestic lifestyle," she finally said. "It's not compatible with our jobs."

Oh, Danielle. "Is that why you couldn't marry Robert?"

Her sigh reached Erin's ears. "I thought I could do it—give up the travel, the glamour, the great pay, the job that didn't feel like work. I loved Robert, and I still do, but while I stood at the altar, I suddenly couldn't imagine settling down on the family ranch, tending animals and probably ending up keeping the business books someday. Maybe taking a trip to San Antonio or Corpus Christi every couple of years." Danielle hesitated, and Erin thought she heard a boarding call announcement.

"Are you in an airport?"

"Yeah, DFW."

"You're leaving Texas already? I thought you might visit with your mom for a week or two."

"No time," Danielle said. "I got a call from a guy who's going to Japan on business for a year, and he needs a nurse. I'm meeting him in Philadelphia. He's taking his wife, teenaged kids and mother. The mom has MS."

Japan?

Her heart thumped, hard. How could this be happening—Danielle getting Erin's dream job?

"Erin? Are you there?"

Her heart resumed a semblance of a normal rhythm. "Where in Japan? Tokyo?"

She pulled in a deep breath, waiting. *Please don't say Osaka... Please don't say—*

"Osaka."

Erin let out her breath, the sudden cramping in her stomach not allowing her to sit here in this rocker a moment longer. She took the steps to the front lawn with its giant oaks. At least, that's what Miss Fannie had called them. They didn't look like oaks, especially with the moss hanging down from their branches.

The cool evening air on her face, along with the laughter she could hear inside the house and in the back, somehow calmed her a bit and cleared her thinking. She'd never told Danielle about Osaka, how her grandparents had served the Lord there back when they were young. Or that Grandma Tucker had willed her nursing pin to Erin and had included a note saying she hoped Erin would go there one day.

She'd certainly never told Danielle that caring for a client in Osaka was her dream job or why Grandma Tucker always had such a huge part of Erin's heart. And she wasn't about to spoil Danielle's trip by telling her now.

"You're going to love it there," Erin said, pushing cheerfulness into her tone and starting for the backyard and its gardens.

Her friend sighed. "I hope so. Especially after I gave up everything for this job."

Gave up everything? "Danielle, when did you get this call?"

Silence.

"Danielle?" This couldn't be good.

"Saturday."

"When Saturday?"

"Remember when my phone rang while we were in the bride's cabin, getting dressed?"

She had to be kidding. "That's when you decided not to marry Robert?"

This made no sense. How could a job offer make Danielle change the whole course of her life? Devastate the man she loved? Break a solemn promise?

And turn her back on a marriage, home, family?

By this time, Erin had wandered to the courtyard. Now she all but plopped into its nearest wrought iron chair and bent over, her elbow on the table, forehead resting in her hand.

"I wrestled with my decision all the way down the aisle."

Oh, Dannie...

"He must hate me," Danielle said, her voice wavering. "But I didn't intend to lead him on. Truth is, I struggled with it from the moment I said yes."

"But you said you loved the idea of ranch life."

"I do! That's what made it so hard. I wanted to marry Robert, to have kids, a house. But something inside me—I don't know. It's like I can't stop drifting. And you know my family history. I sometimes think we're all off balance, unable to stay and make a marriage work."

"That's nonsense." For some reason, Erin panicked a little at the thought of Danielle giving up on ever being married and having a family, probably because Erin had basically done the same. However, Erin somehow managed to keep her voice sounding normal. She hoped. "Just because your mom and grandmother left their husbands, that doesn't mean you can't make a marriage work."

"They didn't just leave. They ran. Like, across

the country. And I'm just like them, Erin, except I'm going to the other side of the world, not just the nation. None of us are marriage or motherhood material."

No, this wasn't right. None of this was right. "You're not thinking it through—"

"You're the last one who should say so." Danielle frowned into the phone, her pretty face marred by fatigue and the creases her grimace pushed into her forehead. "You've been running ever since you broke up with Calum. I always knew you took your first private-duty job with Mr. Dunning because you wanted to hide away from the world in his big house in the Hamptons."

"I worked for Mr. Dunning because he was always going to exciting places. Who else do you know who accompanied a World War Two veteran to the White House? And after he passed, Mrs. Fairchild's offer was too good to refuse. I would never have seen France without her."

Danielle sniffed. "You think you're different than me, but we're just alike."

"No, it's not the same—"

"Wait—where are you?" Danielle hesitated. "Is that Rosewood's pergola behind you?"

Erin winced at her pain-filled tone. She should have used a background, too. That way, she wouldn't have had to tell Danielle she was living at Rosewood—the scene of her friend's wedding that wasn't a wedding. She drew a deep breath, ashamed of having kept the truth from her best friend. "This is where I'm working. For the lady who owns the estate."

"I have to go. My flight's going to leave."

Erin gripped her phone tighter, its edges digging into her skin. "Wait—have you talked to Robert? Is he okay?"

"I can't. He needs to move on. Because I'm not coming back." Her voice grew tight, high-pitched, as if she were holding back tears. "Maybe never."

Before Danielle clicked off, she broke into sobs.

Erin stared at her home screen picture, a shot of herself—alone—in front of the Arc de Triomphe. On their first full day in Paris, Mrs. Fairchild had given her the day off to explore while she rested from the flight. So she'd toured Paris alone.

Just as Danielle was on her way to Osaka alone. Running from commitment, from putting down roots. From love. All because of fear.

Thinking back, Erin remembered Danielle's mom saying once that the women in their family couldn't settle down. And Danielle had believed it, even though Erin had told her at the time that it wasn't true. That she didn't have to follow in her mother's and grandmother's footsteps.

Her friend hadn't listened back then any better than she listened now.

A thought struck Erin like one of Darnell's horseshoes. Was Erin going to end up like Danielle?

She'd never admit to Danielle that she'd been close to the truth about Mr. Dunning and his neighbor, Mrs. Fairchild. Despite what she'd said, Erin knew deep down that private-duty nursing had enabled her to run from her pain, her shame. No one in France knew who she was, and by the time she came back for the wedding, the press and social media had forgotten about her.

But she didn't plan to stay. She had no one to stay for, unless she wanted to go back to New York City and her parents. Which might be a good idea, once she left Natchez.

Not to stay. Just to visit. Because even after three years, she couldn't go home permanently. The pull to get far away was still too strong. She'd been fooling herself, enjoying the pleasant home life at Rosewood, caring for Miss Fannie and Bella and imagining what it would be like to live here forever. It seemed like a charmed life, in a loving household with people she was learning to care for.

But it wasn't her life. She was merely temporary help in a family that wasn't hers. Only a couple weeks, and she'd be gone.

However, if she left again, would she ever settle down? Would she ever return or make a home of her own? No, she'd probably spend her life as a drifter, like Danielle and her mom and grandmother.

Or were the people of Rosewood teaching her she could be something else? Live a different way? Somehow, after talking with Danielle, Erin felt almost as if she'd been given one more chance to change.

Her words to Kiara came back to her. *Christianity is a life of change.* Changing to become more like Jesus. Less selfish. More hospitable, as she'd seen in Miss Fannie tonight.

It was hard for a drifter to be hospitable. Maybe not impossible, but hard.

The back door opened, and Jase and Miss Fannie stepped out onto the gallery, the floodlights now off and the moon shining its light on them.

"Erin?" Jase's strong baritone voice, calling out to her from the warmth of the home, did something strange to her heart. It had been a long time since someone had come looking for her.

"I'm here."

"I was worried about you," Miss Fannie said from the doorway, her hand clasping the crook of Jase's elbow. "I hope you didn't get bad news."

Erin got up and started toward them, their voices of concern still ringing in her ears, warming her heart. "Bad news, yes. Danielle, the bride from yesterday, is running away."

Miss Fannie took her hand as she drew near. "But she already did that, dear."

"This time it's for good. She's probably on her flight to Japan by now."

Inside the hall, she gave Jase a smile of thanks for taking care of Miss Fannie while Erin was on her call, and she took her place beside Kiara for the next round of Hound's Head. Maybe the sweet older lady was more of a friend than an employer, after all.

And Erin was finding, more and more, that she loved Rosewood's warmth. Even more than she loved the charm of Paris.

Chapter Seven

It was both good and bad that Erin was leaving in two weeks. Good because Jase was spending way too much time thinking about her. Bad because he wasn't remotely ready to take care of Bella without her.

He glanced at his watch the next morning. Plenty of time to fix breakfast and have his lesson on how to give a baby a bath before he had to leave for his appointment with the lawyer.

Resisting the urge to let out a groan of despair, Jase pulled on suit pants and a white shirt and peeked into Bella's crib. As he'd done yesterday, he began his day by laying his hand on her head and praying for her—a long, unhurried prayer for her health and growth and for her to learn to love Jesus. And for himself, that he'd get the hang of baby care. Quickly.

Then he allowed himself time to study his

Bible at the desk in his apartment's living room and to pray for the rest of his household, including Erin.

Wow, she'd been a natural with the kids last night. The way she won over every person she met, she might have a calling on her life.

He stopped the thought cold. Whether the Lord had called Erin to the ministry or not, Jase's life would stay the same.

There was something pathetic about a man who'd been stood up at the altar twice and then tried again. No way would he be that guy. By the grace of God and the grandmotherly love of Miss Fannie and his family, he'd survived it twice. A third might not go as well.

So he did what every man did when avoiding woman problems: he went to work.

Trouble was, he worked here in the house with the woman he needed to avoid.

First he placed an online order for a pulldown changing table for the men's room at church. Then he lifted the sleeping baby from her crib, grabbed a pacifier from the basket Erin had put on top of his dresser and covered Bella with a thin blanket. Bella was so tiny, he was afraid to hold her in just one arm. So he left her clean clothes in Miss Fannie's little, old-fashioned dresser and his tie and jacket in the closet and held the baby tightly with both arms.

Instead of thundering down the two long flights of stairs as he used to before Bella came to live with them, he took the steps at a sedate pace. She didn't stir but merely kept her eyes closed and trusted him not to drop her or forget her or fail to find a place to change her diaper.

Jase held her even closer, since dropping her was probably the biggest danger. *Lord, I'd still like to know how I'm going to take care of this baby. Especially after Erin leaves.*

Downstairs, he headed for the kitchen, needing to fix breakfast for Miss Fannie and Erin before going to the lawyer's office to discuss custody and adoption issues. He glanced around for a place to lay Bella, but the table in the breakfast nook didn't seem like a good idea, and the only other option was a countertop. Also bad.

Maybe Miss Fannie was up and he could lay Bella in the cradle in her room. Jase stuck his head out into the hall. Miss Fannie's door was closed. The only other baby-bed options in the hall were the round table and the green velvet settee.

What did parents do when work had to be done, but there was no place to put the baby? The best he could figure, they did the work while holding the child.

That meant he had to hold her in just one

arm. But should Bella's head go in the crook of his elbow or in his hand? He shouldn't have left his phone upstairs. If he had it, he could do a search: "How to hold a baby in just one arm."

Yeah, and if Abe or biker/pianist Zeke or any of the youth group somehow got ahold of his phone and saw he'd searched for that, he'd never hear the end of it.

Best just go with his instincts. Which said to knock on Erin's door and ask for help.

He'd just started for the hall when he heard footsteps.

Moments later, Erin stuck her head in the kitchen. "Okay to come in? I don't want to disturb your genius."

Disturb his—

Oh. She meant cooking. He caught her dimpled grin and couldn't help smiling back. "Funny. Right now, I'm not genius enough to figure out where to put Bella while I fix breakfast."

"Want me to take her?"

Ordinarily, he would hate to admit to a woman that he couldn't do a simple task like this. But his relief was so deep, and Erin looked so cute standing there with her arms out and a sweet smile on her face, he couldn't feel threatened or intimidated.

"Sure. I have this weird fear that I'll forget I'm holding her, and I'll drop her."

"You won't." She took Bella from him and carried her to the breakfast nook table. "No one would guess you'd never held a newborn until a couple of days ago."

Jase took a carton of farm-fresh eggs from the refrigerator and set it on the counter. Then he checked out the rest of the contents and pulled out a red onion, some Havarti, basil and almost a quart of heavy cream. He deposited them on the counter and grabbed a couple of avocados and tomatoes from the fruit bowl by the sink. "Want to learn how to make grits? The best cook in Natchez taught me."

"Miss Fannie?"

He let out a laugh, then checked to make sure his boss wasn't standing in the doorway. "Uh, no. It was Miss Eugenia. Miss Fannie once tried to make supper for herself and her late husband, Colonel Chester, when they were first married and their cook was sick. She says the mashed potatoes were so thin, and the gravy was so thick, the colonel poured his potatoes over his gravy. She hasn't turned on the stove since, or so she says."

Erin's laugh tinkled out like Miss Fannie's silver nurse-call bell. Neither boisterous nor timid, her laugh warmed something in his heart that had frozen so long ago, he didn't know when it had happened.

"What did Miss Fannie say to Colonel Chester?"

A cane tapped against the wood floor outside the kitchen. Miss Fannie, wearing a light blue skirt and a white sweater, came in and sat down beside Erin. "I said, 'I'm going home to Mother.'"

"Did you do it?" Jase asked.

She smiled the smile of a bygone love. "I never could have left the colonel. Especially if I'd realized our time together would be so short."

"You're doing much better this morning, Miss Fannie," Erin said as Bella slept on her lap.

"I am. And I'm hungry for your good breakfast, Jase."

He pulled out the double boiler and poured water into the bottom. "How about some grits and poached egg avocado toast, with strawberries and blueberries?"

She smiled as wide as she always did when he mentioned grits, and she turned to Erin. "I love Jase's avocado toast and his other trendy food, but his grits are so good, they'll make you weep."

"I've heard of them, but I've never had them.

I can't wait to taste some." Erin stood and took a bottle of orange juice from the refrigerator, Bella's head resting in her palm and her little bottom tucked into Erin's elbow.

Huh. So that's how people get work done while holding a baby.

Erin also managed to reach for a glass from the cabinet, pour some juice and hand it to Miss Fannie. "If you'll hold Bella, I can help Jase so he can get to the attorney's office on time."

"That's fine." Miss Fannie gazed at the baby, wistfulness in her eyes, and held out her arms when Erin offered Bella to her.

Jase cracked an egg onto a saucer. Since Erin had made clear her inexperience in the kitchen, he'd better give her an easy job. Although it might be fun to teach her to cook… "Erin, you can rinse all the berries and cut off the tops of the strawberries. We'll serve them in one of the bowls in the china cabinet."

"Jase, the story about the colonel has made me sentimental," Miss Fannie said as Erin began to work on the fruit. "That man gave me everything I ever wanted, including a cook. Even though it meant he had to work longer hours at the department store. And I tried to be as agreeable as possible and make his life as pleasant as I could."

"Your husband owned a department store?" Erin asked.

"It was a small, local store. Chester made a nice living." She made a sweeping motion with her hand, as if encompassing the entire estate. "But this place requires a lot of upkeep. He inherited it, and it's fortunate that he was left a little cash as well. Otherwise, we couldn't have kept Rosewood."

Jase had stirred grits into the cream he'd poured into the top of the double boiler while Miss Fannie told her story, and now he slipped the eggs into the simmering pot to poach. "I'm glad you did. I can't imagine living anywhere else. This is my favorite spot in the world."

At least it would be once Erin had moved on and he felt his heart was safe again.

"It would be sad to lose a family home," Erin said. "Had it been in the colonel's family long?"

"Oh, my, no. Neither of us came from money. A captain in the army left it to him. It seems Chester saved his life during the war, and since he had no living relatives, he left all he had to my husband." Miss Fannie took a sip of her juice. "Have a glass yourself, dear. You, too, Jase."

As Erin poured juice for them both and set the table, Jase chopped tomatoes and avocados and cut the onion into slivers. Then he slid sliced baguettes into the oven to toast. "After the colonel passed on—"

"Went to his heavenly reward," Miss Fannie corrected, pointing toward the ceiling.

"After he went to his reward in 1957, Miss Fannie sold the store to keep this place going. That's when she had the two cottages built in the backyard as temporary homes for pregnant ladies who had nowhere to go."

"I built them in 1959. Things were different then," Miss Fannie said. "Each cottage has two apartments, and I kept them full. Some girls came from here in Adams County, and others from across the river in Concordia Parish."

The giant back door creaked on its hinges, and Miss Eugenia's voice echoed through the hall. "Fannie? It's me."

"We're in the kitchen," Miss Fannie called back.

"Did we leave the doors unlocked last night?" Erin frowned a little, her brows pulling together. "I thought I checked them all."

"I gave Eugenia a key to my house when Chester left us," Miss Fannie said.

Miss Eugenia sailed into the kitchen, clearly on some kind of mission. Then he spied the Mason jar in her hand.

"I promised to bring you a batch of kimchi," she said, unscrewing the metal ring and removing the flat. She set the jar on the table, moved to the silverware drawer beside Jase, and got out a fork for the jar. Then she lifted the double boiler lid and peered in at the grits. "They look just right, Jase."

He reached over and handed her the whisk.

When she'd stirred them, she ran her finger over one of the whisk's wires, scooped up a sample and tasted it. The rare look of approval in her eyes made Jase smile. High praise from the accomplished Miss Eugenia.

"Well done." She rinsed the whisk with the sprayer, dropped it in the sink and patted Jase's shoulder.

"Get a plate for yourself, Eugenia," Miss Fannie said.Then she turned to Erin, who set the bowl of berries in the middle of the table. "He always makes extra in case she pops in for breakfast."

When they sat at the table and Jase had given thanks, Miss Fannie handed the bowl of grits to Erin. "The proper way to eat them is with butter. No sugar, no matter what they told you up north. You'll like them this way."

Jase splashed a little Tabasco on his and waited with way too much anticipation for Erin's response.

She took a bite of the tiny serving of grits

on her plate. Then she smiled and spooned up a nice helping. "I like it!"

Miss Eugenia let out a sigh that sounded like relief. Then she turned to Jase and actually pointed her finger at him. "Jase, as the man of this house, you've been remiss in your hospitality to Erin. She's been here three days now, and I doubt she's seen more than this estate and the church. No one should stay that long in Natchez without seeing at least some of the sights."

Jase wasn't sure he'd exactly call himself the man of the house, since he was an employee here, but he could see her point. "You're right, Miss Eugenia. I've been trying to learn as much from her as I can, so I haven't thought about sightseeing."

"I'm also here to help Miss Fannie," Erin said. "I appreciate the offer, but my place is here at Rosewood."

"Nonsense. Jase, your mama told me she's coming over Thursday night to spend the evening, and that will give you a chance to take Erin around town. I'll come here, too, and between Anise, me and Fannie, we'll make sure all is well."

"Do it, Jase," Miss Fannie said. "I won't have Erin leave without seeing our beautiful town. At the very least, she needs to see the bluff and

Windsor Ruins, since it'll be too late to tour the historic homes. You could take her to a few of them after the wedding Saturday."

Right. He had another wedding to prepare for.

But how would Erin feel about the two of them taking in the town together? It seemed a little too much like a date to him, and she might feel the same.

"I'd enjoy that." Her simple words somehow sounded like a challenge, despite her innocent smile. "Mrs. Fairchild came to Natchez every spring while her husband was alive. She told me about Stanton Hall and its fantastic lunches. I've always wanted to go."

He couldn't hold back a grin. Fine. If she could see the town with a preacher, despite her aversion to them, then he could spend a simple evening with her, too. Especially since he had three days to prepare himself. "Okay, let's start at Windsor and then watch the sunset from the bluff."

Miss Eugenia gave Miss Fannie a split-second glance that Jase probably wouldn't have thought about again if he hadn't recently begun to wonder if she was the mysterious Natchez matchmaker. She caught his gaze then looked away and took a sip of her juice. Probably trying to throw him off track, in case he suspected her.

Which he did.

All his life, he'd heard that, once the mysterious matchmaker had put a couple together, she'd never failed to see the relationship end in marriage. Jase had never believed the rumor. But if Miss Eugenia was the matchmaker, and if she was trying to put him and Erin together as a couple, he had news for her. It wouldn't work. They would be her first failure.

Just as they finished breakfast, Bella awakened. Jase fixed her bottle, and Erin spotted Miss Fannie as she and Miss Eugenia headed toward the parlor bedroom to compose a fundraising letter for their garden club.

Jase gazed down at the baby while she took her bottle. A bath. How was he supposed to give a bath to someone who was too small to put in the kitchen sink?

Bella finished the bottle and gave him a little burp, but Erin hadn't returned. She hadn't said she was coming back, but surely she hadn't left him to figure this out on his own. It wasn't like her. But what was taking so long? Still in his seat in the breakfast nook, he stretched to see into the hallway.

Sure enough, here came faithful Erin, her

arms full of lotion, a pump bottle of baby soap, a towel and who-knew-what-else. "Ready?"

Jase wiped his suddenly damp palms on his pants. "We don't put her in the water, do we?"

"Not until her umbilical cord stump falls off."

Jase knew what the umbilical cord was, but the part about it falling off—that sounded interesting.

She unfolded the towel on the kitchen counter next to the sink, and then laid down a thick, cushy pad. "Lay her on the pad and take off her sleeper and diaper. Then cover her with the blanket. She'll stay warmer if we keep her covered except for the parts we're washing."

Once he had the diaper off, Erin had drizzled a little liquid soap on a soft pink washcloth. "Run it quickly over her arms and trunk. Then I'll give you a cloth with clear water so you can rinse her."

Jase lifted her impossibly tiny arm and scrubbed.

Erin leaned in a little. "Just quickly pass the cloth over her. Babies don't need intense washing like teenage boys do. The longer she's wet, the colder she'll get. We want to keep her warm."

Right. That made sense. "I hope I haven't neglected her by not giving her a bath yesterday. There wasn't time."

"We wash her diaper area with every change, so she needs a bath only a couple of times a week. If we bathe her more often, her skin could dry out, and she could even get eczema."

Jase dried Bella's torso with a soft towel. Then he uncovered her legs and washed them quickly. Was there no end to things that could go wrong if Jase made a mistake? Give her too many baths, and she'd get some dreaded skin disease. Forget to keep her covered up—then what would happen?

"Will she catch a cold if she's not covered?" he asked, his tiny bit of remaining confidence quickly evaporating.

Erin handed him the rinsing cloth. "Probably not. Just do the best you can, and ask me or Miss Fannie if you don't know what to do or how to do it."

Easy for her to say. Jase knew nothing and had everything to learn. And he was smart enough to know he'd need to figure out a new aspect of caring for Bella each time she passed a milestone. What would he do when it was time for shots, when she started to walk, when she went to her first day of school?

He quickly shut down that thought. One thing he'd stopped doing after his rejections was looking to the future, because he had no future. Just his job and youth ministry, day in and day out, for the rest of his life. Which wasn't a bad thing, but he'd learned not to think beyond work. And right now, the hardest work he'd ever done was taking care of this tiny girl, and he wasn't doing a good job. At all.

How would Courtney have taken care of Bella alone if she'd lived? Even if the father was still alive, he might not have been there to help, judging from the kind of life Courtney had said he'd lived.

Erin must have sensed that he wasn't heading in a good direction, because she stepped closer and laid her hand on his arm. "Jase. Take it easy. You're taking good care of Bella."

"I'm not so sure about that."

"You'll have Miss Fannie. As many babies as she had living at Rosewood over the years, she'll know what to do."

Yes, and Miss Fannie was in her late eighties and wasn't in good health. What if someday he didn't have her?

Nothing was certain except the fact that Erin was leaving in a few days. Good thing he'd called Ruth Ann Dixon, the church's nursery director, and hired her to start working as Bella's babysitter next week. Because, the more he thought about it, two other facts were sure.

First, no matter how much Miss Fannie and his family and anyone else helped, Jase was the one responsible for taking care of Bella.

And second, he was going to have a hard time doing it after Erin was gone.

As much as she hated to admit it, Erin wasn't doing a great job of helping Jase feel confident as Bella's dad. Anybody could take one look at the clouds in his blue eyes and see how troubled he felt. The problem was, Erin had no idea how to help him believe he could do the job.

Maybe she was doing too much for Bella and should let Jase take the lead more...

"Oh, no—it's already seven forty-five," he said, a diaper in his hand and his gaze fixed on his watch. "I'm not going to make my appointment with Joseph Duncan. He wants me to bring Bella."

Erin looked down at his bare feet. "I can dress her and put her in the car seat while you finish getting ready."

Rather than relieving the anxiety in his eyes, her words seemed to ramp it up. Maybe she shouldn't have offered. "Do whatever you feel comfortable with," she said. "But in the cool mornings, she needs not only a diaper and dress but also a onesie underneath, and tights, shoes and a hat."

She couldn't quite decipher his expression— maybe sweet confusion. "Go ahead, Jase. It's okay. Even experienced parents sometimes need help."

Jase hesitated then reached out and squeezed her hand. "Thanks."

He gave her the diaper then hurried past her. Within seconds, she heard him barreling up the stairs.

Before she could control it, her heart melted for this broken man.

Instantly, she shoved aside the feeling, recognizing she merely felt sorry that he'd been forced into this impossible situation. And that she had begun to love Rosewood and its quirky owner and even Miss Eugenia.

She quickly diapered the baby, slipped on her tights and onesie, and slid her smocked pink gingham dress over her head. By the time she'd secured Bella in her car seat, Jase bounded into the kitchen, looking far beyond handsome in his black suit and gray tie.

"Erin, thank you. Thursday night we'll take some time to relax a little while I show you Windsor Ruins and the bluff. You've been on duty every waking moment since the wedding, and I should have thought to give you some time off." He paused, and his brow furrowed for an instant as if he was deep in thought. "I just realized how conceited that sounded, as if you'd want to spend your free time with me. You'd probably rather get away from all of us for a while. You can use my car if you want to be alone."

How sweet. "No, I'd like to see the town with you. Unless you have things to do that night or prefer to be alone."

"Nope." He picked up the car seat and Bella and headed for the door. "Wear walking shoes."

In his haste, Jase all but slammed the back door on his way out.

He'd probably no more than left the porch— the *gallery*—when Miss Fannie's little bell tinkled.

Erin secretly smiled at the two older ladies as she started toward the parlor-bedroom. How could they possibly have been more obvious than they had this morning, pushing her and Jase together? She should tell them how fruitless their mission was.

Then again, they seemed to enjoy it, so why spoil their fun? They'd find out soon enough.

"Erin, would you kindly run upstairs and get a scrapbook from my bedroom?" Miss Fannie said from the corner table, where the two ladies sat. Miss Fannie held a notepad and pen, presumably composing their letter to the garden club, Tasha and Sunny sleeping in the sunbeam streaming through the window. "It's the second room on the right. The book is the blue one in the lowboy in front of the window. Bottom drawer."

Miss Eugenia still had that hopeful expression on her face, as if she expected an engagement announcement any moment. What was in that scrapbook, anyway? Surely the two schemers weren't going to show her awkward pictures of Jase as a baby or something equally embarrassing, were they?

Of course not. Even though Miss Fannie seemed like a grandmother to him, she wasn't, and he hadn't grown up here. So she wouldn't have pictures of baby Jase in a diaper or—*please, no*—a bathtub.

"Yes, ma'am," she said and started for the winding stairs.

At the top, she took a moment to glance around the second-story center hall. The same size as the hall downstairs, it had a cozier feel to it, with sofas and chairs that probably dated back as far as the stuffier furniture below. Erin could easily see herself relaxing here with a book or playing a game.

She admitted to herself that the game taking place in her imagination included not only Jase and his family, along with Miss Fannie and

Miss Eugenia, but the youth group, too. Especially Kiara and Darnell—and Chance.

Erin stopped that thought before it could take root. Where had it even come from?

She hurried to the room Miss Fannie had specified—a corner room with the same view Erin had from her room on the first floor. One window faced the front lawn, and the other revealed the camellias Erin loved and had admired just this morning after arising. Best of all, she could see the garden cottages even better than she could from her first-floor room.

Miss Fannie's story of building the cottages for single moms had touched Erin more than she would have expected. She'd noticed a sense of poignancy in the sweet lady's face that suggested she'd had a deep, personal reason for wanting to help those ladies.

Erin eased open the ancient drawer and pulled out a big, old-fashioned scrapbook, the kind her mother had kept when Erin was a girl. She set it on the bed and turned back to shut the drawer.

A silver picture frame on the dresser caught her attention, its black-and-white photograph showing a newborn baby with closed eyes, dressed in a white gown and lying in Bella's cradle. The baby in the picture looked about the same size as Bella, with the same sweet rosebud newborn lips and tiny nose. The lady in the picture appeared to be sitting on the floor, her head resting on the cradle, her hand on the newborn's tummy. She wore black, and her eyes reflected depths of grief Erin had never known.

She caught her breath.

Even though this woman's anguish didn't resemble the contentment Erin had always seen in Miss Fannie's face, there could be no doubt this was her sweet new friend, posing with her only child.

The child she had loved and lost.

Through misty eyes, Erin noticed the silver hair locket, containing a fine blond curl tied with a narrow pink ribbon, hanging from one corner of the frame.

No wonder Miss Fannie had built the garden cottages. And insisted Jase bring Bella here to her home.

Erin took the album from the bed and hurried from the room, casting another glance at that picture on her way out.

Downstairs, Erin gave the album to Miss Fannie, who laid down her pen and notepad and flipped through the first few pages of the book. "These clippings will show the dates Jase wanted, Eugenia."

"The pictures are beautiful," Miss Eugenia said. "I think those first simple weddings were far nicer than the elaborate ones you have here today."

"I've always thought so. Remember my wedding? Pink azaleas from my mama's garden and wild maidenhair ferns. Do you recall driving along the Natchez Trace and digging up a trunkful of those ferns the evening before?"

Since the two ladies seemed lost in their memories, Erin stood to excuse herself. "I'll clean up the kitchen while you reminisce," she said, heading that way.

"Can it wait?" Miss Fannie sounded so disappointed, Erin turned and came back. "I'd hoped to get your opinion about our new Wisteria Chapel advertising. Jase thinks we should include some history on our website."

"I'd be glad to take a look, but I don't know anything about advertising."

"That's all right. I merely want the opinion of a young woman who might plan her wedding one day."

That looked a little unlikely, but…

Miss Fannie patted the chair next to her. "These are clippings from our first wedding ceremony, three years ago. Eugenia, the date was April twenty-seventh."

Miss Eugenia wrote in a notebook as Miss Fannie gave her dates and details of the weddings she had hosted during the past three years.

"Look, Eugenia. Here's a picture of Jase performing the wedding of that famous actor to a model. What was his name?"

"I don't recall. I don't pay any more attention to actors and models than you do. Neither did Jase. He was completely unimpressed with the famous couple and treated them as he would anyone else."

Miss Fannie flipped another page, stopped and laid her hand over a picture. "Oh, dear. I don't know how this got in here."

Please don't let it be Jase in a diaper.

"What is it, Fannie?" Miss Eugenia leaned closer to the album. Then she sat straight up. "It's Jase and Sydney's...well, what do we call it? Attempted wedding?"

Wait—Sydney? "Jase told me a woman named Kayla left him at the altar. Not Sydney."

The two older ladies hesitated, looking at each other as if they'd just spilled a sworn secret.

Erin groaned inwardly, realizing she had just impulsively broken the cardinal rule of private-care nurses: don't get involved with the family's personal affairs.

How could she have done that? Never before had she allowed herself to become so attached to a client and the people around her. And now she'd intruded on Jase's private life as if she were family or a personal friend instead of an employee. "I'm sorry. I forgot myself, Miss Fannie."

When the awkwardness in the room became unbearable, Miss Eugenia pushed out a sigh and pursed her lips a moment. "No, you did nothing wrong. But you're correct that Kayla chose to wait until the middle of the wedding ceremony to break up with Jase."

Miss Eugenia looked at Miss Fannie as if asking whether she should continue.

"Go ahead, Eugenia. She's likely to hear anyway, since the whole town still talks about it."

Talks about what? Erin shifted in her seat. What history had she stirred up?

"Kayla was the first woman who scorned Jase at the altar," she all but whispered, as if afraid Jase—or Kayla—might walk through the door. "Sydney was the second."

No. Oh, no...

Jase. Sweet, humble, compassionate, so-handsome-it-should-be-illegal Jase—jilted twice. Both times at the altar.

For a while, they all just sat there, Erin looking at nothing but listening to the ticking of the case clock, the song of the wind chime outside Miss Fannie's window, the call of a mockingbird.

That explained Jase's initial reluctance to take her to the bluff and the ruins, whatever they were. And the way he'd seemed to look right through the throng of young women at church, even though she could see interest in their eyes. This was why he'd handled Danielle's wedding with such grace and courage, even though he must have collapsed inside, seeing the bride run away.

He clearly knew exactly what to do to defuse the situation as much as possible. Because he'd been Danielle's groom, Robert, standing there with his bride's hand in his, only to have it snatched away. Not once, as Erin had thought.

Twice.

She knew it shouldn't matter to her any more than any stranger's problems would matter—she should empathize, pray for him and go on with her own life. But she couldn't quite do it. He might have been a stranger to her last week, but all they'd been through together had forged in them a bond, the kind that comes from working hard together to meet a common goal. From putting needs of others before their own in order to make someone else's life better. Even from growing to love the same people: these two ladies, Bella, the kids.

Erin wasn't sure when it happened, but at some point, she and Jase had formed trust. Respect. Which made hearing about his heartache—and keeping her own heart safe—all the more difficult.

It was a good thing she was leaving next week, before she could lose her heart completely to Reverend Jase Armstrong.

Chapter Eight

"So this is what all the fuss is about." Attorney Joseph Duncan peered over the top of his black glasses at Bella, a twinkle in his green eyes.

"Fuss is right, especially when she's hungry," Jase said, glancing at the old-fashioned wall clock in his lawyer's reception area. One minute till nine. Another two minutes and he'd have been late. Without Erin, it's hard telling what time he would have gotten here.

"Come back to my office," Joseph said, leading the way with a brisk gait that belied his advanced age. "Your esteemed boss has kept me up-to-date on your situation."

No big surprise, since the two were good friends. If Jase remembered right, they'd been classmates. "I think we're all still in shock. But she's a good baby," he said as he set the car seat on the wooden floor.

In the office that probably looked nearly the same as it had in the days Joseph's great-great-grandfather conducted business here, Joseph waved Jase toward an old straight-backed chair. They discussed the adoption hearing. Then Jase signed about a hundred papers, or so it seemed, between changing Bella's diaper and picking her up when she cried.

"Jase, there's a glitch in the adoption. Bella has a paternal grandfather in a nursing home in Montana—her only living relative on that side. He doesn't feel capable of taking care of her, so we don't have to worry about him making a claim to the baby. And, of course, her maternal grandfather—your uncle—is still in prison." Joseph paused. "However, Courtney's mother has done so."

Jase shifted to lean forward in his seat, his heart pounding. "Her mother? Joseph, Rita has to be at least sixty-five years old. She always called Courtney a change-of-life baby. Rita couldn't take care of Courtney when she was little, so how does she think she could take care of Bella now?"

Unruffled as always, Joseph rolled back his desk chair and crossed his ankle over his knee. "I've seen cases like this before. A relative of an orphaned child or a child whose parents are incarcerated will step up and try to claim a grandchild in order to get foster-parent pay, even though they were negligent or abusive parents with their own children, as Rita was with Courtney."

The old sense of panic hit Jase again, and he drew in a few deep breaths. He recalled a Bible verse he'd leaned on during the time his dad left and the times his fiancées had betrayed him: *My grace is sufficient for thee: for My strength is made perfect in weakness.*

As weak as Jase felt at this moment, that verse had to be true for him.

His throat dry, he tried to swallow. "Courtney wanted me to have Bella. Her mom's a mess, and her health is terrible. The guy Rita lives with is a heavy drinker, and there's secondhand smoke all through their house…"

Jase fixed his gaze on little Bella, who counted on him to keep her safe. He was the man to raise her—he knew it. Somehow, despite all his bumbling diaper changes and attempts to get a burp out of her, he knew he was the one both Courtney and the Lord had chosen to raise Bella. "What are we going to do?"

"If she pursues it, we'll go to court," Joseph said as casually as if he'd said they were going to the river bluff to watch the sunset.

My grace is sufficient…

"I don't have money to go to court. Miss Fannie pays me with an apartment, food, the use of the colonel's Mustang and a small check every week. And since you're a deacon in our church, you already know what I make there. Zero."

Although he'd been offered a salary, he'd refused it, following the Apostle Paul's example.

"Don't let that concern you. Rita probably won't follow through. If she does, we'll worry about it then. With her history and her current illness, we can make a case for you to keep Bella. I have an interest in this case, so I'll give you a break on my fees."

Yeah, Jase had heard that before, when businesses had sued Mama for payment of the debts Dad left behind when he took off. It meant Joseph was going to charge nothing. But they'd see about that. Bella was worth any cost, and Jase was willing to pay it, although he'd probably have to make payments for years. "What can I do to make sure Rita doesn't get custody?"

"When the court appoints a guardian, it always looks to protect the best interest of the child and considers the child's overall life. CPS will do a home inspection and determine whether the home is a safe and suitable environment in which to raise a child. So look around Rosewood and see if it's safe and suitable."

"How will I know?"

"Get Miss Fannie and your nurse to help you. Look for anything that might be a hazard. Start with that winding staircase y'all have there. It's beautiful, but it's a hazard. Get a baby gate and tell the social worker you'll use it once Bella starts crawling."

It would take a lot more than a baby gate to get rid of Jase's uneasiness about this whole situation. "I don't understand why it's even an issue. Courtney made a will when she found out she was pregnant, and she named me Bella's guardian."

"A will has some value in this case." Joseph made a grunting sound as he returned his documents to the antique upright file cabinet in the corner.

Jase knew that grunt. It always meant a lecture would follow. Joseph had earned the right, having helped Jase's mom throughout the years. But now he looked too serious, even for a lawyer.

Joseph returned to his chair, his eyes a little too solemn for Jase's comfort. "Miss Fannie and I have been good friends since our school days. So when she's troubled, I'm troubled."

Please don't let this be about Miss Fannie telling Joseph I'm a total knucklehead when it comes to babies...

"You remember that I raised four children on my own, including Carol, to whom my Frieda was giving birth when she died."

"I've heard that, yes." But honestly, he'd never given it a thought. "I can't imagine having a newborn and three other children, too."

Then it hit him. Joseph had words of wisdom that would help Jase raise Bella. "What advice do you have for me, sir?"

"No advice. Just a caution."

Caution—to keep from somehow accidentally causing harm to Bella because he was clueless about babies? Or to make sure he didn't overwork Miss Fannie, since she wanted to be involved in Bella's care? Or a dozen other things he could think of…

"Your boss is concerned about you, and so am I."

Naturally. "I admit I'm having a hard time taking care of—"

"This isn't about the baby. It's about you."

"Sir?" Jase didn't know which to be more surprised about—the fact that Joseph, the most proper Southern gentleman he knew, had just interrupted him or that the baby wasn't his biggest concern.

Joseph leaned back in his chair and stroked his famous white mustache. "Not many people are still alive who remember that Miss Fannie was once my fiancée."

Wait, what?

Jase had known Miss Fannie and Joseph as long as he could remember. But he'd never heard a word of this.

"I trust you not to talk to her or anybody else about this. I was her schooldays sweetheart, and Chester Swan was a newcomer to Natchez at the time. She struggled to decide between us."

Miss Fannie and Joseph Duncan? No couple he knew seemed less suited.

Then again, he hadn't known Colonel Chester. The colonel might have been even less like Miss Fannie than Joseph was.

"Our relationship felt comfortable, safe. But Chester made Fannie come alive. I bowed out as gracefully as I could, seeing how perfect they were together." Joseph drew his brows together as if in deep thought. "For years, I buried myself in work, unable to find anything else to catch my interest or attention. Then one day, I thought about Chester and how he always seemed full of life, enjoying every moment of every day. I looked at myself and concluded that Chester was the better man. Not because of his personality or character, but because he'd been hurt before, too, but he kept fighting. Kept driving himself toward the life—and love—he wanted."

"And you fell in love again," Jase said, seeing depths of the elderly man that he'd never noticed before.

"With fear and trembling, yes." Joseph turned and gazed out the window, the one that faced the backyard. Jase looked, too, at the spot where Mrs. Duncan had created one of the most popular stops in the garden club's annual tours. The space had come to life with camellias and snapdragons, tulips and pansies, just as the gardens had at Monmouth.

Joseph had kept fighting...

"I'm not going to pry into your love life, Jase," Joseph said, swiveling in his chair to face him again. "But I will say I've watched you since you experienced your own heartaches, and I'm not sure you kept up the fight after those women betrayed you."

No, he hadn't. "I can't see trying a third time."

A spark lit in Joseph's eyes. "I'm not talking about women. I'm talking about other things that matter. Besides working for Miss Fannie and the church and helping your brother with Rock Steady Boxing at his gym, what do you do?"

"Well, I cook..."

"We all cook. What else?" At Jase's hesitation, Joseph stood and looked down at Bella. "She's a big responsibility. She needs someone who will fight for her. Not bury himself in work and neglect her—and other important things. Like relationships."

Yes...

"Which kind of man are you?" Joseph said. "A fighter or not?"

Jase hesitated. He knew which man he wanted to be. But he didn't know if that was the man he was.

He shook Joseph's hand, picked up his daughter and went home to find out.

Lord, please don't let us miss anything.

Thursday afternoon, after spending much of the day helping Jase work on the new Wisteria Chapel website, Erin walked through Rosewood's main floor with Jase and Miss Fannie, looking for potential hazards. The baby gate stood ready against the wall, between the piano and the stairs. The home was clean and smelled good, as it had since Erin arrived, and all knives and sharp objects were put away in the kitchen. And of course, Miss Fannie didn't allow clutter or tripping hazards in her home, and the robot vacuum took care of dog fur. She couldn't think of another thing to check.

"I'm still concerned about the stairs," Erin said as they looked up at the beautiful yet slightly dangerous steps. "Having Bella sleep on the third floor might make the social worker nervous, especially since this staircase is so long and narrow. The fact that it's curved won't help, either."

"Then let's move Jase and Bella down from the third floor to the second floor." Miss Fannie led the way into the kitchen and sat in the breakfast nook. "What do you think, Jase? Let's discuss it over fruit salad and lemonade."

With Bella sleeping in the parlor-bedroom, Jase grabbed the Tupperware container of fruit from the refrigerator while Erin carried glass bowls and spoons to the table.

"Would the social worker and judge think Bella would be safer in a second-floor apartment, Erin?" Jase asked, spooning fruit into their bowls.

"I don't know. It's possible." Erin stirred the fruit in her bowl. "I assumed the only apartment in the house was on the third floor."

"It's not exactly an apartment," Miss Fannie said. "It's a suite—a bedroom and a sitting room. An apartment would have a bathroom and kitchen, like the one on the third floor. But on the second floor, the bathroom is down the hall. And, of course, we have a kitchen right here."

"The sitting room could be Bella's room," Erin said. This idea was beginning to make a lot more sense than carrying Bella up and down two long flights of stairs.

"And I won't be sleeping upstairs for a while," Miss Fannie said. "In fact, I think I'll keep my bedroom down here permanently and continue to use the hall as the parlor."

But maybe Jase liked his third-floor apartment. Erin glanced at him to gauge his reaction to Miss Fannie's idea.

To her mild surprise, he looked relieved.

"I like it. We'll all live in a big home instead of Bella and me living in an apartment within the house," he said. "Of course, if you decide to move upstairs again, we'll think of something else."

"Fine. If you leave one guest room, you can use all the others." The light in Miss Fannie's eyes revealed how much she wanted the social worker's approval. "Let's move you tomorrow."

"I'll call all the muscle I know," he said, a twinkle in his blue eyes.

Then it hit Erin: if the social worker decided Rosewood wasn't a safe and suitable place for Jase to raise Bella, they'd have to move out.

And from the looks of things, Jase didn't

want to move any more than Miss Fannie wanted him to.

With the housing issue settled for now, Erin took a long drink of her lemonade. It seemed each batch Jase made tasted better than the one before, if that was possible. Always on top of his game, he seemed to give as much as he could to the people he loved, and making perfect lemonade for Miss Fannie was just one way he loved his people well.

"Better wear something warm to go sightseeing this afternoon, Erin. There'll be a breeze on the bluff." Jase paused, eyeing her cropped pants and white tunic. "If you still want to go."

She couldn't tell if he hesitated because he'd rather not take her or because he didn't know if she wanted to go. Or for some other reason altogether.

"Sure, but if you're tired, we can stay home," she said, giving him opportunity to bow out.

"I haven't been to Windsor Ruins in several years. I'd like to go." Jase stood and put the fruit back in the refrigerator.

By four o'clock, when the doorbell rang, Erin had changed into jeans and a lightweight blue sweater and was waiting for Jase to come downstairs. With Miss Fannie in her room with the door shut, Erin let Miss Eugenia and Jase's mom, Anise, inside.

Moments later, he came downstairs, holding Bella in one arm, his other hand skimming the stair rail. The sight warmed her, especially since she'd been praying for him to start to feel more comfortable with the baby.

He handed Bella to his mom, and then it felt as if he rushed Erin out the door. When they started down the long, winding drive, he glanced over at her, his smile a little shy. In the afternoon sun, his eyes turned a brighter blue than she'd seen before—a beautiful shade that seemed somehow to suit the man he was inside.

"Windsor Ruins is near Port Gibson, north of here and close to the river. We could get there faster on the highway, but I like to take the Natchez Trace because it's prettier. It's a scenic drive through protected land, and a lot of it looks the same as it did four hundred years ago."

Twenty minutes into their drive on the Trace, Erin had to admit Jase was right. Their slower pace on the two-lane road felt just right after her busy days of caring for Bella and Miss Fannie and helping with the household's daily needs.

The Trace held simple pleasures, like natural beauty, groves of trees and grassy meadows, with no billboards, no semis or other commercial vehicles and little traffic. "This feels like a vacation," she said as they passed a herd of deer.

"Whenever I have to go to Port Gibson or Vicksburg, I use this road. I'm always relaxed when I get there. Partly because the speed limit is only fifty. To me, driving slower is more restful."

She couldn't hold back her giggle. "Says the man who drives a Mustang."

Jase's smile looked soft, thoughtful. "This car still officially belongs to Miss Fannie. It was the colonel's."

The notion brought a sting to her eyes. "She loves you, Jase."

He nodded. "She's like my mama. She loves well."

Erin drew a deep breath and forced a smile, suddenly needing to lighten the mood. "Was the car a Christmas gift?"

He shook his head. "Miss Fannie's resources are limited, and the car was one way she could keep me on as her estate manager. We deducted the amount I would have spent on a car payment from my monthly pay."

When they turned off the Trace onto the highway to the ruins, Erin felt a pang of disappointment. Surely the sights ahead couldn't compare to the peacefulness of the old road.

"Windsor was one of the most spectacular homes in Mississippi," Jase said as he opened her door for her. "You're going to love it."

Suddenly, she hoped she would. This place seemed important to him, and if she didn't find it as stunning as he did, would she disappoint him? Realistically, there was little chance the ruins would live up to his fascination. Erin didn't like to think she was jaded, but in her travels, she'd already seen some of the most stunning architecture in the world. How could piles of rubble compare?

The moment she saw Windsor Ruins, she realized how wrong she'd been.

Remote and silent, with no sound but the song of the wind in the trees, Windsor evoked the distant past with its twenty-three remaining giant columns and its ancient Southern live oaks surrounding the ruins. A sense of fragile permanence wafted through the relic, with cast-iron Corinthian capitals still topping the remaining columns even as their bricks crumbled and fell to the ground as chips or dust.

No, nothing she'd seen in Paris had compared to this.

Hearing Jase walk up beside her, she realized she'd forgotten he was there, absorbed as she was in the beauty and tragedy of Windsor. "I have no words, Jase. The home itself gone, with grass growing in its place, but the columns refusing to fall down and die—I've never seen anything like it. I want to weep at its demise and yet I can't, although the beauty that remains is so poignant."

He nodded, a not-quite-smile in his eyes. "I can't feel sorrow at its destruction when I'm here because its resilience is so strong. Look at those columns. How have they stood for over one hundred and twenty years after the fire that destroyed the house? They seem determined to stand, to live."

"I can't find words to describe them."

Jase stopped, looked into her eyes. "It's like trying to describe love."

He drew in a tremoring breath, and she wasn't sure if the shakiness was because of the awe-inspiring overwhelm of Windsor or because he so feared the word *love*. At least, in a romantic sense.

"We can walk the perimeter of the home site," he said, moving closer to the ruins and breaking the mood somewhat. "Stay behind the fence, because the columns are in a state of decay, and debris is always falling. This place is beautiful and inspiring but also could be dangerous."

Dangerous? But how beautiful would it be to see the ruins from within the square of columns? To imagine visiting Windsor at the height of its glory and climbing its now-missing stairs to enter the home and experience its grandeur and beauty? Pretend to dance in its ballroom with the love of her life?

Besides, she didn't think any bricks would fall or columns suddenly collapse, having stood there over a century.

She nodded toward the grassy center. "Take the risk."

Chapter Nine

Instinctively, Jase knew Erin wasn't talking about the risk of getting hit with a stray falling brick. She was talking about their hearts.

He couldn't refuse Erin, partly because she'd clearly loved this place at first sight, as he had, but also because she understood how he felt about Windsor. About uncertainty. About loss and risk.

And now, experiencing Windsor with her, he couldn't be honest with himself unless he admitted that he cared for her. More than that—*Lord, help me*—he'd begun to have deep feelings for her.

She stood here, next to a stately column, the breeze blowing wisps of her pretty blond hair across her cheeks and the sun turning it to gold. He knew taking her hand and stepping among

those columns with her now was more dangerous than standing there during an earthquake.

He didn't want it. Didn't want to fall in love.
Didn't want to take the risk again.

Nope. He wasn't going to do it.

He just had to wait it out. A week from now,
Erin would leave, and he'd never see her or hear
from her again.

Although she did love Miss Fannie, so those
two would probably stay in touch, and Miss
Fannie would tell him what she wrote in her
letters…

Yeah, he was in big trouble.

Jase clasped her hand, the feel of it sending
something sweet through his heart. He stepped
over the rope and inside the ruins with her, sa-
voring the softness of her hand in his.

"This is where the lady of the house greets her
guests." She led him farther into the "house."

He should have dropped her hand and resisted its pull on his heart. But he couldn't bring
himself to do it, no matter how much he might
regret it in the future. "Is the mistress of Windsor having a party tonight?"

"She's throwing a ball to celebrate the birth
of her beautiful new daughter. This is the center hall, with a grand staircase over there." She
gestured toward the opposite "wall" and started
toward it.

"Parlor on the right or left?" he asked, beginning to get into the spirit of the game.

"On the left, beyond the study. Just like Rosewood." She turned to look at him, as if to watch his reaction. "And the dining room and kitchen on the right. In the parlor sits a cradle where a little dark-haired girl takes her naps."

He smiled. "You miss Bella, don't you?"

Erin's eyes softened. "I do."

I do. The words he'd longed to hear from two women, whose names he could barely remember as he held Erin's hand, looked into those brown eyes that took his breath and cleared his mind. "I do, too."

"You'd like to start for home, wouldn't you?"

"I promised you a river sunset." A part of him wished to escape Erin's beautiful eyes and secret himself away in his apartment. But for the first time, thoughts of hiding from rejection made him more miserable than before. Hadn't he already spent the past year that way? "If we leave now, we'll get back to Natchez in time."

"I'd hoped to find an old coin or button or something," Erin said, dropping his hand and bending over to poke around in the ground with a stick lying beside them. "I guess that was unrealistic."

"People come out here with metal detectors all the time. I doubt we'd find anything." It was the truth, although probably not what she wanted to hear. Crushing her hopes of a souvenir made him feel a little like a lout.

"That's okay. I've been looking forward to seeing the river, too."

On the way back to Natchez, at times when she could get a cell signal, she pulled up a website describing Windsor's history and read to him some interesting theories about the fire and its owners. She seemed to sense the struggle within him and wanted to help him relax.

It almost worked.

When they got back to Natchez and pulled into Bluff Park, the red-roofed gazebo sat empty, looking out over the river. "There's the best spot to watch a sunset."

They got out and crossed the strip of grass just wide enough for the Natchez Bluff Trail, some picnic tables, trees, viewing scopes and a few old-fashioned streetlights.

As the sun dropped and dusk approached, the sky turned a fiery red and they climbed the gazebo's nine steps. Inside, Erin leaned against the frame and gazed toward the south, where the sky deepened in hue and reflected in the water below. "I never dreamed the river would be so beautiful. I wish I could live right here on this bluff, looking out at this view every day."

"There are some houses on the bluff, and a few bed-and-breakfasts with great views."

"Maybe I'll have to rent one someday." She paused, looking out at the expanse of water that separated Mississippi from Louisiana. "The sunset glows here, doesn't it?"

Jase had never thought of it that way but yeah, it did. "I've always loved sunsets, ever since I was a kid."

He shouldn't have let that slip. Because he didn't want to think about the long-ago evening Dad took off, leaving Jase with a ray of the setting sun as his only companion…

"Jase, where did you just go?" Erin laid her pink-nailed hand on his as he gripped the gazebo's rail.

He snapped back to the moment. "What do you mean?"

"You left me for a moment there, and it looked like you went to a bad place in your mind."

At first, all he could do was look at her, soak in the compassion in her eyes. No sympathy, just caring…

"I'm okay. Just remembering something."

She stepped a little closer. "It must have been something pretty bad, because you were shaking."

Shaking… He gripped the rail with the hand Erin still held. He shook that night, too.

"Jase, have you told anyone about this event?"

"Mama knows. And Pastor David."

"What happened?"

"It was the night Dad left us. He didn't pack a bag and tell us goodbye. As far as I know, he took nothing with him." His voice came out rough, deep. "Mama had to work second shift at the nursing home—she was a nurse's aide back then. I was seven, and we had a kid's ministry event one Saturday afternoon. Mama dropped me off before work, and Dad was supposed to pick me up later."

He tried to smile a little to soften the details. "He never showed up. He just left me there. Later, we found out he took off driving until he hit the West Coast. All the other parents had picked up their kids, but no one came for me. Even Abe was gone because he was spending the night with a friend."

"So you waited for your dad."

He nodded. "I heard one of the church ladies ask someone whether my dad was going to pick me up or leave me there. Now I know she meant that as a joke. But I was just a little kid, and I got scared. For whatever reason, I thought I should hide. So I sneaked into the choir room and hid in the robe closet."

"How'd you know there was a robe closet?"

"I'd been there with Mama when she was getting ready to sing."

"And the church ladies thought your dad had picked you up," Erin said, her voice soft.

"Right. After they all left, I was in the church by myself for what seemed like hours, roaming around the Sunday school rooms, playing and eating the snacks I found there. Until the sun started to set. Then I got scared."

He paused, unsure whether to go on. But for some reason, he wanted her to know what had happened to him that night. "Pretty soon, it was dark in the church. So I went to the foyer and sat on the floor, watching the sunset through the entry doors until I fell asleep. I don't know why, but it was comforting."

When Erin remained silent, her head bowed, he instantly regretted telling her. No doubt she thought he was overly dramatic or self-focused or—

"What happened then?" Her sweet voice, filled with compassion, could break his heart if he'd allow it.

"About midnight, the lights clicked on. Apparently, when Mama got off work at eleven and Dad and I weren't home, she called the ladies who were working the kids' event and finally figured out what happened. So she went to Pastor David's house and dragged him to the church." He drew in a deep breath and blew it out, hoping to settle the quivering in his stomach. "Erin, I'm sorry. I usually love sunsets because of that night, when it comforted me. I don't know why it almost put me in a panic tonight."

Erin tightened her hold on his hand and dropped her voice to a whisper. "Maybe because you're afraid you'll fail Bella."

Of course. "It seems inevitable—"

"Every parent fails, but your dad chose to fail. There's a difference. You'll never hurt Bella on purpose."

The tiniest glimmer of hope lodged itself in his heart. "No. I'll never choose to hurt her or reject or abandon her."

"I also think you pour yourself into those kids because that's what you needed when you were a child. If someone had taken time to make sure you were okay the night your dad left, you wouldn't have experienced the trauma of being locked in the church, alone." The concern in her face could rip his heart in two. "Jase, you're keeping these kids from being alone."

Suddenly, as his shard of hope grew, he remembered all the other times Erin had known what nugget of truth to give him, what knowledge to impart, what encouragement he'd needed. Like the time he panicked in the hospital parking lot when they'd gone to get Bella. And when she'd taught him how to put the baby in the car seat and how to feed her. Most of all, he remembered how she was on his side, believing he could raise this child, encouraging him and knowing he'd succeed.

Ever since Erin came to Rosewood, she'd been there for him, always giving herself for him, for Bella. Even for Miss Fannie and the teens. It seemed nearly every moment, she was there, supplying what he lacked. Knowing what he needed. Completing him.

Before he could change his mind, he drew closer. "Erin—"

He brought her hand to his chest, watching, looking for a sign that it was okay…

Erin tilted her head slightly, moved a fraction closer. Slid her eyes shut.

And he kissed her. There in the gazebo, with the waning sun turning everything around them to a rosy glow, with the gentle river breeze cooling his cheeks and swirling her lilac scent around them, between them.

She tasted of lemons and sweetness and things unsaid but understood, things he'd never dreamed he could share with someone like her. And when she kissed him back, it seemed so right that he pulled her closer and let himself imagine that he could fall—

Oh. But he couldn't. Because he was still a preacher. And she was still leaving.

He pulled away, rested his forehead against hers. "Erin."

She pulled in a deep breath and let it out slowly, breaking away from him. "I—I shouldn't have—"

"No. Don't say it." He knew exactly what she wanted to say, and she was right. It was foolish to play around with emotions this way when they knew it would come to nothing. He took both her hands and just held them, memorizing the face and the touch of the girl he could easily have fallen in love with.

Erin had barely closed her eyes the night before, remembering Windsor Ruins and how she and Jase shared a love for its haunting beauty and history. Not to mention his childhood trauma, the sunset on the river and his kiss.

Mostly his kiss. And the quiet ride home.

But wow, what a kiss.

While comparing men's kisses didn't seem quite proper, she couldn't help it. Nothing about Calum's kisses ever brought a sense of emotional connection the way Jase's had. It could have been the perfect ending to a perfect evening, if only things had been different.

If she wasn't leaving.

If Jase wasn't a preacher.

Looking back on the past week, she wondered for the first time if she'd been mistaken—if some preachers didn't let the ministry separate them from their wives, their kids. Living here in the house with Jase and Miss Fannie, she'd never noticed him neglecting the older lady. Just the opposite, actually.

She'd have to give this more thought. Hopefully not in the middle of the night again.

Late that afternoon, Darnell helped Jase make spaghetti to serve the teens before tonight's Valentine's Day play practice while Erin helped Kiara dust the second floor as her grandmother vacuumed.

"Those youth group boys made a mess while they were moving Pastor Jase's and Bella's stuff downstairs," Kiara said over the roar of the vacuum in the second-floor center hall. "I don't think they even wiped their feet when they came in the house. It's a good thing me and Mamaw are here to clean up after them."

"That's for sure." Erin ran her feather duster over the harp in the corner, admiring its graceful lines and cherry finish. "The boys saved Pastor Jase and me a lot of work, though. If the school's water pipes had to burst, today was a good day for it to happen."

"And I got to help Mamaw all day and make some more money." She dropped her dusting rag and pulled her phone from her jeans pocket. "I'm saving up to buy this for my mama's birthday."

Kiara scrolled until she found what she wanted then handed the phone to Erin.

She gazed at the picture of a silver mother-and-daughter necklace with two entwining circles and a poem about a mother and daughter's love. "Kiara, it's beautiful. Your mom's going to love it."

"Yeah." She slipped the phone back into her pocket. "I miss her. A lot."

Hearing the wistfulness in the girl's voice, Erin missed her own mother, too. Running from her family suddenly failed to give her the comfort it once had. If it ever really did. Erin had talked to her mom only once since she got to Rosewood. She'd make time to call her tonight.

They moved to Miss Fannie's room next. Since the parlor-bedroom was full, they'd left the rest of her furniture here, so the room looked the same as it had when Erin discovered the baby's picture.

Starting at the door, Kiara began dusting

counterclockwise. "Will you do her dresser? I hate to do it."

Erin flicked her duster over the dresser. "Why don't you like it?"

"That picture gives me the creeps. The one with Miss Fannie touching the dead baby."

Erin glanced at the framed photograph. "How do you know the baby is dead?"

"Mamaw told me so. She says Miss Fannie's baby was dead when it was born, and her husband was already dead, so she couldn't have any more."

So Erin had been right. Miss Fannie's only child had died. Compared to what she'd gone through, Erin didn't have any problems.

She'd just lifted her feather duster to the brass chandelier when her phone rang.

Danielle. "Kiara, it's my friend from Japan. I'll be right back."

Erin stepped out into the hall and swiped the screen to answer. Sitting propped up on her pillows in bed, wearing buffalo-plaid pajamas, her dark hair tousled, Danielle looked as if she hadn't gotten up yet.

"Hey, isn't it about five in the morning there?" Erin crossed the center hall and headed toward the door to the second-floor gallery.

Danielle yawned. "Six. My boss's mom is an early riser."

Erin laughed as she went outside and down the stairs to the ground. Anything before ten was early for Danielle.

"We're catching a plane for Thailand this morning. I wanted to call before it's time to help Mrs. Sinclair get packed and ready." She flung back her covers and swung her legs over the side of her bed. "When's your last day at Rosewood?"

"A week from tomorrow."

"Where are you going?"

"Not sure yet. I've had a couple of offers, but neither one seems right."

"Then think about this. A guy from Minnesota is coming to Osaka to work with Mr. Sinclair for a year, and they have a toddler with spina bifida. They have two other children, too, and they want a live-in nurse. I told Mr. Sinclair about you. He wants you to interview for the job."

Erin stopped in the courtyard, a rush starting in her heart and surging through her body. "Dannie, is this a joke?"

Danielle drew the phone close to her no-makeup face, her puffy eyes, her messy bun gone bad. "Do you think I'd get up this early and call you looking like this if I was kidding?"

Erin laughed, suddenly missing Danielle so much, it hurt. Despite all her quirks, Dannie had been the best friend to her that she knew how to be.

Something had shifted in Erin in the past few days, and now, for the first time, she wanted her friend to know her deepest longing, and her desire to share it outweighed her fear of others discovering that her dad hadn't been her only dysfunctional parent. "There's—there's something I've never told you."

Danielle's stunning green eyes widened, beautiful despite their puffiness.

"Remember when my mom gave me my grandmother's pin at our ceremony?"

"How could I forget? You were the only one in our class to get two pins."

"Most people think my mom inspired me to become a nurse. But that's not true. Grandma Tucker was my inspiration." The words tumbled out fast, maybe because Erin was afraid she'd lose her courage. "I never wanted anybody to know this, but my grandparents were missionaries to Japan. They answered the call when I was eight."

Danielle sucked in an audible breath. "And they lived in Osaka, didn't they?"

"Right."

"Why didn't you ever tell me?"

Erin sighed, her explanation suddenly seeming flimsy, even in her head. "I was ashamed because, after my grandparents moved to Japan, Grandma Tucker mothered me better from Asia than my mom did from home."

"How'd she do that?"

"Mostly by mail. We wrote letters back and forth several times a week. She kept up with what was going on in school, with my friends, even with boys. I told her about my struggles and my girlish heartaches, and she asked me questions and showed interest in everything I was doing." The memory drew a smile from Erin. "And she was always sending me little presents."

Danielle pulled her phone away from her face and propped it up on something, maybe a pillow. "That doesn't explain why you never told me they were missionaries. I always thought they lived close to you."

"I'm not saying it makes sense. But all my life, work came first for my mom. It seemed like every time someone called in, she went to work. No matter what was going on in my life or how many shifts she'd already worked that week. She always said 'yes' to work and 'sorry' to me." Heat rose in Erin's face as she revealed the secret of her childhood home life. "Which means I had an absent mother and an unconcerned father. And who wants to broadcast that the only person who showed them love in a meaningful way was a grandparent on the other side of the world?"

The way Danielle slowly nodded, then dropped her gaze, made Erin realize her friend knew what it was like to have a loved one move so far away.

The revelation twisted Erin's gut as she paced the courtyard's brick floor. Had she been so absorbed in her own pain that she couldn't see that Danielle, of all people, could sympathize?

Apparently so.

"The year they came home on furlough, they lived with us. They always took me along to the churches they visited to raise support. It was the only time I felt like I had a real family." Erin realized she still had the duster in her other hand, and she flicked it over the top of the nearest courtyard table as if she could also flick away the painful memories of her past. "I always wanted to visit Grandma in Osaka, to relive the moments when she made me feel loved. My dad always said we'd go someday, but work always got in the way, and Mom wouldn't let me go alone. I always thought I'd go after college, when I was on my own. But both of my grandparents passed away during my senior year of high school, so I never got to go."

"Do you still want to come to Osaka?"

Erin laid down the duster then pondered

the question as she stepped onto the grass and gazed out over the back lawn with its wisteria-covered pergola and rose gardens. "Are you kidding? Osaka is my dream job. What's the deadline for applying?"

"Monday morning. Which is your Sunday night."

"I'll let you know."

When she'd hung up, she heard footsteps behind her and turned around.

It was Jase, holding his kitchen shears and the small basket he always used when he picked herbs for a meal.

"Sorry. I didn't mean to…" He took a step closer. "Job offer in Japan?"

She nodded, her throat tightening at the sight of his eyes—vulnerable. Maybe a little crushed. "Yeah…no. It's just an interview. For a job in Osaka."

Comprehension dawned in his eyes. "Your dream job. I guess you want to take it."

How should she answer that? Of course she wanted to take the job. It was Osaka.

And yet…

What would she do if Jase would ask her to stay? To continue living here at Rosewood with him and Miss Fannie so they could get to know each other better?

Even ask her eventually to become Bella's mother?

Maybe things would be different than they'd been with Calum and her dad. What if all ministers weren't like them? More important, what if Jase wasn't like them? Other than the incident during the church prayer, she'd never yet seen him leave to meet someone else's needs instead of Bella's. Could Erin have blown that situation out of proportion?

Although she'd known Jase only a week, she honestly felt she knew him. Because unlike her relationship with Calum, she'd been with Jase almost every waking moment. She'd been fortunate to see Calum for a couple of hours twice a month.

She'd need to think about this. Maybe even talk to someone. Somebody other than Danielle, of course. As much as she loved her friend, Erin had never gotten the best advice from her.

"I don't know," she said honestly. "You're right. It's my dream job. I'll have to see what the client wants before I can decide." *And what you want.*

Because, standing there in Rosewood's courtyard, Erin realized she'd fallen in love with Jase. Not as she had with Calum. Until now, she hadn't realized how shallow her emotions had been toward him. Her former fiancé's betrayal had been more about hurt feelings than a broken heart. After their breakup, she hadn't missed Calum. She'd merely missed the security of having someone.

The heart is deceitful above all things, and desperately wicked: who can know it? The Bible prophet Jeremiah had been right. It had taken Erin several years to discover the depths of her own heart when it came to Calum.

"I don't know what to say." Jase fiddled with the shears in his hand, casting his gaze across the expansive lawn. He opened his mouth as if he wanted to say something, but the back door slammed and Darnell came out. "We need that basil for the sauce pretty soon."

The moment having passed, Jase closed his mouth and handed Darnell the shears. "You know which one is basil?"

"Sure." The boy started for the herb garden, a distance away but still too close for them to continue the conversation.

"Maybe you can tell me more after youth group," Jase said, his voice deep and low and lilting, almost musical in its drawl.

She could listen to this man's so-romantic voice for the rest of her life.

At the sound of tires crunching the gravel in the drive, Jase turned away. "The rest of the kids are coming. I'd better let them in so I can get back to the kitchen and supervise the spaghetti sauce."

"I'll do it." She shooed him inside as Darnell came toward them with the shears and so much basil, he could have made an herb bouquet. "Go in and save supper."

He nodded his thanks and turned toward the house.

Had she just said "supper"? Jase's Southern dialect must have rubbed off on her more than she knew.

And maybe more than her speech was changing. Because, although she'd never thought it could happen, Erin had finally begun to open her heart once more.

Chapter Ten

No matter how hard Jase tried, he couldn't forget the longing in Erin's voice when she'd said Osaka was her dream job. Which meant he had to admit he had fallen for her—hard.

That didn't mean he knew what to do about it. If she hadn't gotten that call, he might have hoped she'd stay and learn to love him. To trust him to be sensitive to her needs while still shepherding the people the Lord had given him to care for.

But now his hope faltered. Soon, when they had that talk about the job offer, they'd need to discuss two subjects, each as important as Osaka: the ministry and her mistrust of pastors.

Until then, he had a meal to finish for the teens.

At the kitchen counter, he sharpened his best knife then grabbed a handful of freshly washed basil leaves. He rolled them tightly to chiffonade them for the spaghetti sauce and ran his knife through them, creating delicious little ribbons. As he sliced, he tried to imagine life at Rosewood without Erin and her kind heart that made sure everybody around her had everything they needed. Without her encouraging, sweet smile.

Without her kiss.

He'd better not let his mind go there now.

That kiss had seemed natural, almost planned somehow, as if it had to happen. And she'd understood his need to keep kids safe. Didn't that mean she understood ministry?

He rolled up another stack of basil and ran the knife through it as if he was slicing out all his inadequacies and doubts about Erin and Bella. While he was at it, he might as well deal with his anxiety about Miss Fannie and Rosewood itself, too, since both of them depended on him to keep them safe, financially stable and strong. He grabbed more leaves, rolled and attacked them, creating tiny little strips of basil, their aroma filling the room as he sliced.

Maybe he should have somehow resisted kissing her. That would have been difficult, since he hadn't given it any thought before jumping right in. Now that he thought of it, what was the matter with him? Jase Armstrong didn't go around kissing women he didn't intend to have a serious relationship with, if not marriage. In fact, he hadn't touched a woman since his last wedding fiasco.

As he stacked more basil leaves, he realized he hadn't considered one important fact: the very real possibility that Erin didn't share his feelings and might never love him no matter—

"Pastor Jase, are you gonna put all that basil in the sauce? I thought you wanted to freeze some for later."

What? He looked up at Darnell, then glanced down at his mountain of basil chiffonade.

He groaned. He had to stop thinking about Erin in the kitchen. "Uh, no. Go ahead and get out the ice cube trays and freeze most of this in some spring water."

Jase separated a reasonable amount of basil and was about to toss it into the sauce when he glanced up again.

Darnell hadn't moved. "You okay, Pastor?"

No. "Yeah, I'm fine." He glanced at his watch. "Go ahead out to the hall and make sure all the furniture is cleared to one side of the room so we can rehearse the play, okay?"

"You sure?"

If a thirteen-year-old boy could pick up on Jase's lovesickness, things could get bad once he got out there with the other kids. He needed to get a grip. "I'm sure."

Once Darnell had left the kitchen, something didn't sound right in the hall. Jase stopped to listen—and heard nothing.

A dozen teenagers, completely silent?

He'd better get out there, now.

Jase ditched his white apron and rushed to the kitchen door. There he stopped, unable to believe what he saw: the entire youth group sitting cross-legged on the floor, Erin standing behind Chance with her hands on his shoulders, leading the kids in prayer. Even from this distance, Jase could plainly see the boy's black eye and fat lip. Another fight in school, no doubt. But this time, Chance's troubles seemed to have driven him to prayer. For the first time, as far as Jase knew.

He swiped his hand over his face, swallowing back the lump growing in his throat. How had this happened? He'd never seen his teens praying as intensely as they did now.

Miss Fannie sat on one of the sofas off to the side, Bella in her arms and the dogs at her feet. She kept dabbing her eyes with a Kleenex as if she was at somebody's funeral.

Jase crept over and sat beside her.

"Erin's a natural with the youth group," she whispered.

Yeah, that went without saying.

It was time to start rehearsing the play if they were going to get a good practice in before they stopped for supper. But the way the kids were connecting with the Lord in here, Jase didn't want to cut the prayer short. So he sat next to Miss Fannie and waited, back where he could oversee the event without intruding, and added his own silent prayers to those of the teens.

Finally Chance stood, breaking the mood. "Thank y'all for praying for me and my mom," he said, swiping his sleeve across his eyes.

Jase decided to give the kids a few minutes to transition from their deep prayers to a more lighthearted time of rehearsal. "If anybody wants lemonade or a Coke before we run through the play, help yourself in the dining room," he told them, then checked his watch. Five minutes should be long enough.

The kids scattered, all but Chance, and left him and Erin alone where the impromptu prayer meeting had taken place. Within moments, their chatter and banter filled the house as usual. Funny how young people could bounce from deep prayer, even tears, to silly jokes in about half a second.

Sunny and Tasha moved to Miss Fannie's bedroom, no doubt due to the noise.

Jase brushed his hand across Bella's soft

cheek as she slept. "Are you good with holding her a few more minutes?"

Miss Fannie swatted his arm, grinning. "Do you need to ask?"

"Nope. Just don't want to wear you out."

Erin came over and sat next to him, her subtle lilac scent wafting toward him.

"What just happened here?" Jase asked.

She was beautiful tonight in her jeans and white sweater, her golden hair loose and silky-looking, a little pink lipstick on her lips. He tore his gaze from her mouth, focusing on her rich brown eyes in an attempt to keep from thinking of their kiss.

Before she could answer, Chance came over and stood there silent, looking at the floor. Wow, his eye and lip looked even worse close up.

Erin patted his arm, her cheeks damp with freshly shed tears. "He prayed for forgiveness of his sins and asked God to do His transforming work in his life."

"Chance—that's amazing." Unsure why he was always surprised when the Lord answered his prayers, Jase stood and gave the teen a quick hug, not wanting to embarrass him. "What happened to make you want to do that?"

"It was— Something happened at home tonight." He swiped at his eyes with his sleeve again.

"Sit down," Jase said as Erin scooted over close to Miss Fannie, making room on the big sofa.

To his surprise, Chance stepped around Jase and plopped down right beside Erin, leaving Jase to sit on the end. If ever again he heard Erin say she wasn't qualified to do youth ministry, he'd remind her of this moment and this boy who trusted her.

"Tell me what happened," Jase said. "I'm guessing it had something to do with the condition of your face."

The boy touched his swollen lip, and for a second, the old surly expression crept into his eyes, like he was about to clam up. He fisted his right hand and twisted it—hard—against the palm of his left. "Yep."

Before Jase could respond, Erin laid her hand on his. "It's okay," she said, her voice as gentle as when she spoke to Bella. "I'm proud of what you did, and Pastor Jase will be, too. Go ahead and tell him."

"Gene was my mama's weasel-face boyfriend, back when we lived in Tupelo. They had a baby, Misty, and we had to keep her quiet when Gene was home. Because he's mean and abusive."

"Tell him about Misty," Erin said, her voice little more than a whisper.

He drew in a big breath. "She was only a week old. Early in the morning, Mama went to Misty's bedroom to check on her, but she wasn't breathing. Mama tried to revive her, but it was too late. When we got home from the hospital, Gene started blaming Mama, saying she should have checked on her earlier, should have laid her in her crib different, stuff like that. Then he started yelling and pushing Mama around, and he finally hit her."

A cold wave washed over Jase, his stomach suddenly cramping. He reached out and squeezed Chance's shoulder.

Chance looked up at Jase, his eyes red-rimmed and wet. "I ran out and called nine-one-one, but before the police got there, he was gone. They never found him. Mama and I moved down here to live with her sister because we never wanted to see Gene again. But this morning he found us. He wanted money, but Mama wouldn't give it to him, so he hit her. I called nine-one-one again, just like before, but this time I didn't stay on the phone. I pulled him away from Mama, and then me and Gene got into it."

"Is your mama okay?" Jase asked, not sure what else to say.

"She says she is."

"Where's Gene?"

"In jail."

Bella woke then, made a little squeaking sound and looked up at Miss Fannie, her blue eyes wide open. In an instant, Jase knew what to do. He got up and lifted the baby from Miss Fannie's lap, then turned and handed her to Chance.

The boy cuddled Bella gently against his chest, and as the tiny girl gazed into his eyes, she seemed to soothe something in his heart. "Bella, you're sweet like Misty. Her eyes were blue, too," Chance whispered.

His eyes burning, Jase cleared his throat and called the other kids back into the room to practice the play. When they'd settled down a little and Jase had taken a few deep breaths to steady his emotions, he had them stand in their places, as they'd been practicing for the past month.

Kiara raised her hand. "Can Chance be in the play? I know he doesn't have a part, since he just started coming to youth group, but we could make up a part for him."

"Great idea," Jase said. "What do you say, Chance?"

"Sure." He grinned and gave Bella to Erin.

"Everybody, pay attention," Jase said as chatter began in the group. "Start thinking of a part for Chance. I'll be right back."

He opened the basement door next to the kitchen, went down the steps and soon came back up with a whiteboard, marker and stand. Within moments, he had the board set up and snapped the cap off the marker. "Character ideas, please."

As the kids shouted out ideas for Chance's part, Jase wrote each random thought on the board, no matter how silly. Before they'd narrowed down the list, a knock sounded on the front door.

Erin stood to get it, so he turned back to his board and his kids and kept working. Ten minutes later, all the teens wanted Chance to play the part of Lester, a young, dorky bachelor pastor who'd given up on love.

Jase gave them the goofiest look he could muster. "This might sound random, but is your bachelor pastor supposed to be me?"

"No, because you're old." Chance mimicked his expression so perfectly, Jase had to give in.

"Everybody, bring your scripts into the big dining room so we can write in Chance's character." Then Jase remembered the visitor at the door. "Get pencils out of the buffet drawer and jot down some ideas for adding Pastor Lester to the play, and I'll be there in a minute."

Then, on second thought, "And nobody touch your phones while you're in there."

He turned toward the sofa where Erin and Miss Fannie watched the teens scramble to the dining room. There he saw dark-haired Yolanda Coleman, the new social worker who'd recently moved to town and who attended his church, sitting beside Erin and chatting with her and Miss Fannie.

"Miss Yolanda, I'll bet you're here to see Bella," he said, carrying over one of the chairs from the round table.

"She's a beauty," she said. "I'm here to make sure y'all are taking good care of her and to see that the home is safe and appropriate for a child. But first, what have you got going on here, with all these kids?"

"I called a special youth-group meeting to-night," Jase said, settling into his chair in front of her. "The church Valentine's party is next week, and we're practicing a play."

"Good. I bought my ticket last Sunday, so I look forward to it." Miss Yolanda looked around the room. "I'm sorry that I need to tour the house while you're having a youth group meeting."

"Jase, I can take the kids while you show her around," Erin said. "If Miss Fannie doesn't mind holding Bella. Or I can put her in her cradle."

"I'll take her," Miss Fannie piped up, holding out her hands.

Miss Yolanda laughed. "The first thing I'll write in my report is that you have plenty of loving caregivers who are eager to help with the baby."

Yeah, but one of her caregivers wouldn't be here much longer.

"There's a lot of love in this old house, Jase," she went on. "It looks like you have everything under control."

"Well, between Miss Fannie stealing Bella's heart and Erin stealing the hearts of my youth group, I'm just the guy who makes the pizza and spaghetti around here."

By the time they finished their tour, the social worker had seen everything from Jase's old apartment to the basement, including his office and the lobby area for the bridal parties in the rear wing.

"I'm happy that you moved to the second floor, Jase," she said at the front door.

Just as Erin had said.

When Miss Yolanda was gone and he had changed Bella and laid her in the cradle, he peeked in the dining room. No big surprise that Erin had the teens under control, adding Chance's lines to their scripts.

If only the rest of his life could be just like tonight...

Why couldn't Erin see what a natural she was with the kids—that the Lord might be calling her to it? What would it be like to have a helpmate in the ministry and his home, adding vibrancy and love to the work he'd started? Expanding it, deepening it. Making it more fruitful. He could imagine Erin growing in her faith and becoming settled, leaving behind her habit of running as far from home as she could.

Maybe Erin had a calling and knew it, but she didn't want to admit it. All Jase knew was that, if she wasn't leaving for Japan in about a week, which he was sure she would, she might have made the best youth pastor's wife in Mississippi. Not to mention the best nurse Natchez had ever seen.

He couldn't think that far ahead, though, because if Jase were to consider getting engaged again, his fiancée had to know she was called to ministry. He should have made that rule before he met Kayla and Sydney. If he had, he could have avoided a lot of pain.

He took a moment to listen to the kids' ideas for adding Pastor Lester to the plot. Then, since neither Erin nor the teens had noticed him, he backed out of the dining room and into the kitchen to heat the water for the pasta.

Because tonight, that's who he was. The pizza and spaghetti guy.

And for tonight, that was enough.

Early the next morning, joy seemed almost tangible as Rosewood prepared for another wedding. This time, Erin got to be a part of it—and not as a bridesmaid. The entire estate buzzed with anticipation and vendors as the wedding hour drew near.

"I forgot to pick up my suit." Wearing athletic pants and a long-sleeved blue T-shirt, his feet bare, Jase pounded down the spiral staircase.

Erin smiled at his habit of going barefoot in the winter. But in Natchez, February felt like spring to her. "What do you want me to do? Go to the cleaner's or stay with Bella while you go?"

"Neither." Miss Eugenia glided into the house, unruffled as always and carrying what looked like a bakery box. "I'll get it for you. Jase, the florist is here. She's looking for you in your office."

He looked down at his feet. "I can't meet her like this."

Miss Eugenia raised a brow as she took in

his disheveled, rather adorable appearance. "What happened? Did you oversleep? I trust those aren't your pajamas, since you're parading around the first floor in them."

"Bella started getting fussy at about five this morning." He looked at his watch. "I guess I fell asleep in the rocker with her."

"Tell me what to do, Jase, and I'll handle the florist while you change," Erin said.

"But my suit—"

Miss Eugenia shoved her box at him. "This is spinach quiche and mixed berries from Rosemary's coffee shop. Take it to the kitchen and eat, then put on your blue suit for now."

"Yes, ma'am." He took the box. "Erin, did you eat?"

"I'll grab something later. Give me instructions for the florist, and I'll—"

A loud cry from the second floor cut her off.

Jase set the box on top of the piano and turned toward the stairs. "I have to get Bella first."

"You eat. I'll get Bella," Erin said. "Miss Fannie is dressed and sitting in the kitchen waiting for Miss Eugenia, so she won't need me. When I get back downstairs, I'll take Bella to your office to meet the florist."

He took her hand. "Thanks. I—I can't seem to get along without you."

Something in his beautiful eyes made her think he wished to say more, but after a moment he grabbed the box again. "All the wedding instructions are on my desk in a black folder labeled 'Meriwether Wedding.'"

"Got it."

She started up the stairs, but he stopped her with a hand on her elbow. "Erin, when I said I can't get along without you, I meant it. I don't like the thought of you leaving."

Was that his stress speaking, or his heart? How could she respond, since she didn't know?

Bella let out another wail, so Erin just gave his hand a squeeze and sprinted upstairs. When she reached the suite, she headed straight to Bella, whose little fists shook with her cries. "Poor baby, upstairs all alone."

She kissed Bella's soft cheek and then sang little songs as she changed the soiled diaper and put on a fresh pink sleeper, the baby still crying. Then Erin grabbed a matching hat and a pacifier, wrapped Bella in a blanket and picked her up.

The moment she held the infant to her chest and swayed with her a little, the crying stopped. Erin shifted her to look at her face.

Bella gazed into Erin's eyes and flashed a tiny, split-second smile.

Oh, sweet, motherless baby, giving me your first smile...

Her throat tightened as her eyes filled, and she wanted nothing more at that moment than to hold this baby and love her. To comfort her.

To be her mother.

She didn't pretend to know how Jase felt about her. He'd said he couldn't get along without her, but that wasn't the same as loving her. But now that she knew she loved Jase, and she'd known all along that she loved Bella, it didn't seem right to leave. Not just yet. Because how could they move toward a relationship if she lived thousands of miles away?

If this ceremony turned out like the last one, Jase was hanging up his Wedding Preacher hat.

However, he saw no sign of a cold-footed bride—or groom—so he forced himself to relax and enjoy the moment. Miss Fannie wanted to stay in the house and watch Bella instead of her usual habit of attending the weddings held at Wisteria Chapel, and Miss Eugenia stayed behind with her. Erin, however, sat in the last row of chairs, as he'd asked her.

For the first time, he admitted he wouldn't mind if she was his date for a lot more Wisteria Chapel weddings.

While the thought scared him a little, it felt

right to have her here, encouraging him with her presence.

Could she be thinking the same thing? Would she enjoy dressing up in the pretty pink dress she wore today and go with him to the symphony in Vicksburg? Or take an evening jazz cruise with him on the steamboat *Natchez*? Funny how every time he thought of Erin, he thought of pink.

He glanced at her when he should have been looking at the bride. As beautiful as Erin was today, he wouldn't be surprised if all the guests thought she'd outshone the bride.

Could she care for him, even just a little? If her kiss had meant anything at all, he might have a sliver of a chance.

Jase pulled his attention back where it belonged, determined as always to put his whole heart into his work, despite the cute distraction in the back row. "Dearly beloved…"

He did a fine job of concentrating until he got to the couple's vows—the hardest part of the ceremony for him. Both his attempted weddings had ended before this point, and he'd never gotten the chance to say *the words*.

"Do you take this woman to be your wife, to live together in holy matrimony, to love her, to honor her, to comfort her and to keep her, in sickness and in health, forsaking all others for as long as you both shall live? If so, please respond by saying…"

He paused, glanced at Erin.

"I do."

Jase dragged his gaze from her before her wide brown eyes and sweet smile distracted him to the point that he'd lose his place in the ceremony.

And maybe even lose his heart.

Chapter Eleven

There was something inherently wrong with Valentine's Day falling on a Monday.

Somebody needed to declare it a national holiday. That way, a man would have enough time to take his lady on a proper date. A special date. A date that involved a picnic on the river or dinner at a nice Cajun-Creole restaurant. Or visiting the ruins of an old mansion that somehow spoke to them both through its haunting beauty.

Regardless, this Valentine's Day was on Monday, and before heading to church for the party and play, Jase lifted Bella's little foot and slipped on her white sleeper with red hearts, which Mama brought over last night. His baby looked at him with those big eyes, almost as if she knew who he was and was pleading with him not to leave her as Courtney had.

Could babies remember things that had happened to them during their first days? If so, did Bella remember that she'd been alone after her mama died? Well, not alone, because nurses were always with her. But the one person familiar to her had left her forever.

Then he remembered the first time he held her, the way she'd responded to him. Yes, Jase believed Bella could remember. He snapped her sleeper then picked her up and held her close, hoping to comfort her. "I won't ever let you be alone again, sweetheart."

He meant to keep that promise, to keep Erin at Rosewood. Because Bella had only three familiar people left in her life: Jase, Miss Fannie and Erin. By the end of the night, he hoped to call Ruth Ann and tell her he didn't need her babysitting services after all.

He went to his dresser and picked up the card and necklace he'd bought for Erin today. It might be corny, but he'd selected a heart pendant on a silver chain. He slid them into his messenger bag, along with the play script, and took the stairs at his new sedate pace.

Downstairs he found Erin and Miss Fannie in the kitchen packing up the salad, prime rib and roasted red potatoes he'd made for church. They'd filled three insulated bags already and were working on numbers four and five. "You kept some out for your supper, right?"

"Yes, and Bella looks adorable in her valentine sleeper." Erin zipped her bag and then held out her hands for the baby. "You come to me and let Daddy get his keys," she said in that sweet, quiet way she had with Bella.

The baby stretched and looked as if she was reaching for Erin, making them laugh.

"I dressed her up for Valentine's Day, even though she doesn't get to go to the party." He turned the baby over to Erin. "I wish all three of you could come tonight."

"Don't worry about us," Miss Fannie said. "After supper, we'll eat candy hearts and drink lemonade and have a fine time at home. Or maybe we'll go to the Malt Shop for ice cream."

"And watch *Sense and Sensibility*," Erin said. "The most romantic movie ever."

Hmm. Jase didn't know about that, but it sounded like a chick flick to him. Maybe he and Erin would watch it together next Valentine's Day.

He grabbed his keys from the hook inside the pantry and carried his messenger bag and the bags of food to the back door. Then he backed Miss Fannie's SUV out of the garage, in case they decided to go to the Malt Shop. He pulled his car out, loaded up and headed to church.

Two hours later, Jase carried the last of the leftovers into the kitchen and started toward the teen Sunday school room to give the kids their final instructions for the play. He was about to pray with the teens and send them to the basement fellowship hall stage when Pastor David came in, his phone in his hand and his brows furrowed.

He motioned Jase to the hall, then shut the door behind them. "Miss Jessie called. She's on duty at the ER tonight, and they just brought her granddaughter in. Hailey overdosed again."

What? "I thought she was in rehab."

"She checked herself out last night and ended up in ER tonight."

"Is she okay?"

Pastor David shook his head. "They're life-flighting her to Jackson as soon as she's stable enough. Miss Jessie is holding everybody together right now, as she always does, both in the ER and in her family. But she needs support."

Jase let out a groan. "I haven't seen Miss Jessie since we took Miss Fannie to the hospital. But I called her Saturday night, and she said Hailey was doing great."

"We both know how these things go."

Unfortunately, yes. According to their new policy, Jase made evening pastoral calls, due to Pastor David's Parkinson's, so it was time to head to the hospital.

Then he stopped. Was Erin right, that pastors didn't always have the correct priorities? He'd always run toward the most urgent need, just as Erin said her father and fiancé had.

Maybe it was time to stop doing ministry his way and instead seek the Father's will in each circumstance.

"If this had happened two weeks ago, I would have taken off for the hospital without giving a second thought to the teens," Jase said. "I always thought they were solid and stable enough to handle it. But recently, something happened that changed my mind about the way I do ministry."

Pastor David glanced toward the youth room door and smiled at the ruckus inside. "Do you mean you're going to start doing the hard work of discovering the Lord's will in each situation, instead of having a blanket policy that tells you to drop everything and run, no matter how it affects the people in your life?"

Well, when he put it that way... "Uh, yeah. I guess so."

"I had to learn that lesson, too, about forty years ago. Start with getting the teens' input." He glanced at his watch. "Best get at it."

Right. "Give me just a minute with the kids."

Jase breathed a quick prayer, headed back into the Sunday school room and told them about Hailey.

"I need to go to the hospital. They probably won't let me see Hailey, but Miss Jessie needs me. I want to know how you feel about this." Jase paused, let his gaze land on each teen. "I can stay until the play is over and then go to the hospital. Or I can leave now and be there sooner for Miss Jessie. Y'all know her because she's here every time the doors open. Some of you older ones remember Hailey, too. I need to visit them and pray with them, and I need to decide whether to go now or after the play."

For a moment that felt like an hour, the kids stood silent, some with eyes closed.

"Go to the hospital. Now." His tone insistent, Chance pointed at the door.

A week ago, Jase never would have guessed Chance would become a leader in the youth group. "What do the rest of you say?"

"Go. We know what to do," Kiara said, and the others agreed.

"Yeah, I'll have my foster dad record it for you," Darnell said.

"Y'all are awesome, and I'm proud of you." Jase swallowed hard. It'd been a long time since he'd had to fight back tears as often as he had this past week. "Go on backstage, and I'll have Pastor David tell you when to come out."

He stepped back into the hallway. "Did you hear that?"

"I did. You're teaching them right, Jase."

Jase didn't know about that, but he knew seeing his teens maturing this way felt great.

He ran to his car and sped toward the hospital.

It was time to face facts. The way Miss Fannie grew stronger each day, she no longer needed a private nurse. That meant Erin would soon be out of a job and couldn't stay here much longer.

"Miss Fannie, I've enjoyed my time at Rosewood so much, I haven't wanted to think about the future," she said as they settled in for an evening of prime rib and a movie in the hall. Bella was fed and happy in her cradle, which one of the boys had brought out yesterday from what they now all called Miss Fannie's bedroom.

"Then don't think about it. Enjoy the moment." Miss Fannie took a bite of Jase's prime rib and closed her eyes, making little humming sounds. If anyone knew how to enjoy the moment, it was this dear lady. "Maybe Jase will propose, and you can keep living here with us."

Knowing Miss Fannie, she should have expected an answer like that, but somehow it took her by surprise. She hesitated, wanting to choose her words wisely. "It might be better to have a plan. A job and a place to stay."

"Eugenia is always saying things like that to me. But I say we have a happy home here, with you and me taking care of Bella and Jase taking care of Rosewood. You're a big help to Jase in the ministry, too."

Erin had to admit she'd been enjoying the teens. "Still, I'll have to move on. It'll be hard to give up Bella, though."

"It's always hard to give up a baby." For the first time, Erin saw pain in Miss Fannie's eyes. "Back when I opened my home to the unwed mothers and their babies, I grieved each time one of them moved out."

Opened her home? "You mean opened the garden cottages, don't you?"

Miss Fannie's eyes widened. "Oh, my, no. They slept and showered in the cottages, but they ate and spent the evenings here. They all had jobs—that was a requirement—and my volunteers and I took care of the babies here in this home. I didn't leave them holed up in the little cottages."

Interesting. "What did you do in the evenings?"

"I taught them to be homemakers—how to keep house, sew, do laundry, keep a checkbook. All the things a mother should teach her daughter. When I opened the garden cottages, I soon found out many of them had no idea how to clean or organize a home. And if they did, they helped teach the others." She took a long drink of lemonade. "Of course, Eugenia had to teach the cooking."

Of course. "Maybe you could open the cottages for single moms again someday."

"I would love that."

"Why did you close them?" Erin asked.

"Oh, I got old. And so did the volunteers. Then I had to close the cottages when I got pneumonia three years ago. I never did completely bounce back from that. But later, when Jase moved in, I felt like I had a purpose in life again, giving him a place where we could both extend hospitality to the teens. And to anyone who needed a good meal and some companionship and encouragement. Jase and I—we needed each other."

"I can see how you needed help, but what did Jase need?"

She sighed, pushed back her plate. "Someone outside his family to love and care about him, to help him recover from the shock and pain of his second wedding falling through."

"Right. Anyone would need love and compassion after going through the experiences he had."

"He's doing much better now, except for the way he keeps such distance from women. Until he met you, of course."

Erin decided to let that comment pass.

"When Sydney left him at the altar, it destroyed him. His brother, Abe, found him in the home Jase and Sydney bought together, just sitting there in a kitchen that had never been cooked in. He'd been there two days. Abe hauled him out of there and over here to take care of me. He's been at Rosewood, watching out for me, taking care of the estate and being the Natchez Wedding Preacher ever since."

Wow. Erin had known Miss Fannie had the gift of hospitality ever since the moment she walked in, but who knew she could bring a heartbroken man back to a place of normalcy?

"You lost your baby here, too, didn't you?" She touched Miss Fannie's hand. "I saw the photograph on your dresser."

Miss Fannie smiled, her eyes soft. "Little Evelyn Grace. She was stillborn, right up there in my room. It was four months after my Chester died."

"I don't know how you managed—"

A knock sounded at the door, and Erin rose

to answer, checking the shelf clock on the round table. "Who would come here now, at eight o'clock on Valentine's Day?" She strode down the hall to the entrance and opened the door.

A skinny, stringy-haired woman about Miss Eugenia's age stood there, wearing a stained white sweatshirt and dated-looking jeans. The stale odor of cigarettes clung to her, although she had portable oxygen strapped over her shoulder and a cannula in her nose. "I need to talk to Jase."

Could this woman be here because she needed help, like the people who used to come to Erin's house when she was a child, asking for assistance with rent or groceries? If so, she didn't want to turn her away...

Erin opened the door wider but still stood at the threshold to prevent the woman from walking in. An old Buick sat in the winding front drive, engine running, hubcaps missing and a dent in the passenger door. A man sat behind the wheel, watching.

Something didn't feel right about this. "I'm Erin Tucker, the nurse here. May I ask your name, please?"

"I'm Rita Armstrong. Courtney's mom," she said. "I need to see Jase about the baby."

Erin looked back at Miss Fannie, who shook her head almost imperceptibly.

She turned back to Rita. "Jase can't come to the door right now. Would you like to come back tomorrow?"

"Sorry, that won't work. I've come all the way from Vicksburg to take my grandchild home."

Take Bella away? She couldn't be serious. Erin turned and looked behind her again. Miss Fannie had picked up Bella and was heading for the kitchen with her. "That's impossible. You can't take her."

"I'm her grandmother, and a grandmother is closer kin than a second cousin. I have a right to her."

The man opened his door and got out of the Buick. Big and bald and wearing a tank top that revealed more than it covered, he looked as if he could crash right through a locked cypress door if he chose. He stood in the driveway, clearly here for muscle power, and stretched, his huge biceps bulging.

Jesus, help me protect Bella from these people...

"I can't do anything, because I'm just the nurse. Wait here and I'll give Jase the message."

"You better do it fast," the man said, a threat in his voice. "We're taking that baby with us."

Was that a handgun in the waistband of his jeans? Erin couldn't be sure. She swung the door shut and turned the key. Then she raced to her room to grab her phone. She dialed Jase on her way to the kitchen.

The call went straight to voice mail. He must have turned off his phone for the church party.

She slid her phone into the back pocket of her jeans so she could call the police as soon as she had gotten Bella to safety.

A fist pounded the front door. "Bring us the baby or I'm coming in for her," the man yelled. "I'm not leaving without her."

"Miss Fannie, we have to get out of here. He could break the window and come in before the police could get here."

"Where?"

Erin hesitated. "The church. Jase has to handle this. And there'll be lots of people around, so they won't try to snatch her."

The older lady looked out the window toward the service driveway behind the house. "My car's in the back driveway. Jase must have pulled it out for us in case we decided to go out for ice cream, to make it easier since Bella's along."

"Get the car keys. House key, too." Erin ran to the hall and grabbed Bella's car seat and a blanket. She dashed back to the kitchen, strapped Bella in and threw the blanket over her. "Go!"

Outside, she locked the door, then held the car seat with one hand and Miss Fannie's arm with the other as they hurried to the courtyard and then to the car.

Erin secured the seat while Miss Fannie got in the back seat beside her. She raced around the SUV and got in. Started the engine.

"Take the service drive instead of the front drive," Miss Fannie said. "When we get to the road, they'll see us, but we'll have a head start."

Erin threw the car in gear and gunned it.

They reached the highway in moments. "Left or right?"

"Left on Quitman."

That meant they were doubling back and would pass the house.

"They're halfway down the drive," Miss Fannie said. "Left is faster."

Her heart pounding, Erin turned left.

"Do you know the pastor's phone number?"

"No, and I didn't bring my purse, so I don't have my phone."

Erin shifted to grab her phone out of her back pocket and passed it over her head to Miss Fannie just as Bella started to cry.

"Call nine-one-one and put it on speaker."

When dispatch answered, Erin opened her

mouth to speak, but Miss Fannie was faster. "Marsha? Is it you? This is Fannie Swan."

"This is Marsha, Miss Fannie. What's your emergency?"

The woman who'd answered when Miss Fannie passed out the day of Danielle's wedding.

"This is Erin Tucker, Marsha," Erin raised her voice over the baby's cries. "I'm Miss Fannie's nurse and I live at Rosewood. We have a child abduction attempt. We got away from the house, but the abductors are following us. We're headed to… What's the name of the church, Miss Fannie?"

"River Church," she shouted.

"We need the police, Marsha. Jase is at the church, and we're taking the baby there."

"I'm sending a car now."

"That's it, right up there," Miss Fannie said.

Erin laid on the horn to get someone's attention in the church as she sped into the parking lot, and she didn't let up until she stopped at the entrance. She flung open the door and ran around to Bella. "Get in the church, Miss Fannie," she shouted.

As she unfastened the screaming baby from the car seat, Chance raced out of the church. "What's going on?" he yelled.

"Abduction attempt. Help Miss Fannie in the church!" Erin snatched the baby from her seat.

While Chance helped Miss Fannie, Erin ran with Bella to the church, holding her tight, the car doors still flung wide. The piano player from yesterday—Zack? Zeke?—opened the foyer door for her and waited there for Miss Fannie and Chance.

The Buick pulled in behind them, and the driver's door opened.

"Do you have a key to this door?" she asked the piano player.

"Yeah, I'm a deacon."

"As soon as Miss Fannie's in, lock it! Those people are trying to abduct Jase's baby."

"Got it."

"Then lock down this building. Lock every door." She peered into the sanctuary. "Where is everybody?"

"In the basement fellowship hall," Chance hollered from just outside the foyer.

"Keep everybody down there."

Once Miss Fannie was in and the door locked, the piano player ran down the stairway off to the right, Chance and the elderly lady following. "I'm on it." His voice began to fade. "Pastor, there's a problem upstairs."

At once, the pastor appeared. "What's going on? Something wrong with the baby?"

"Attempted child abduction. Take Miss Fannie somewhere safe and keep everybody in the fellowship hall. Then tell Jase that I have Bella."

"Jase isn't here."

"Where is he?"

"He left right before the play and went to the hospital to visit—"

"No!"

It was happening again…

Erin didn't wait around to find out Jase's excuse. It was up to her to keep Bella safe.

She ran with the crying baby to the brightly lit sanctuary and looked for a place to hide.

The door near the front, the one Jase and Pastor David had used when they came into the sanctuary at the beginning of the service on Sunday—where did it lead? She ran toward it, pushed it open.

A narrow hallway.

Erin flipped on the light and slowed her pace until she reached the middle of the long passageway. There she sat on the floor, leaned against the wall and cradled Bella. If Rita or her muscle opened the door on either side, she'd have a half-length advantage.

"Poor baby. You poor, poor baby," Erin murmured. She caught her breath and held Bella close, rocking her, trying to comfort her, to no avail. She kissed the baby's cheeks, rubbed her back. Her wails didn't stop.

But they had to stop. If Rita had somehow gotten inside before the deacon had all the doors locked, she'd hear Bella, and she'd walk right in with her goon and take her.

At least, she'd try. Because Erin would never give up, never let them have her.

Her fear was probably prompting Bella's crying, so she took deep breaths, prayed and tried to calm herself. Having no pacifier, Erin wiped the pinkie of her left hand on her shirt, trying to remove any dust or dirt. Then she crooked her finger and placed her knuckle in Bella's mouth like a makeshift pacifier.

To her relief, the baby took it, her little tongue and gums working Erin's knuckle.

It wasn't the most sanitary thing she'd ever done, but desperate times called for desperate measures…

Still on the alert but somewhat relieved to hear sirens outside, Erin felt her pulse slow to a more normal rate. With Bella quiet now, she had time to think.

The first thing she thought of was Jase.

Absent Jase.

To be fair, he had no idea Rita would come and try to take Bella, so she couldn't blame him for that. But he'd left the kids before the play started and gone to the hospital to visit who-knew-who.

And let the teens down.

Did he not realize how much tender care Chance needed now? And Darnell had the lead part. How could Jase go off and make a hospital call when the kids needed him?

If he'd been here tonight, where he was supposed to be, he could have helped her protect Bella. But no, it had happened just as it had with Calum, years ago. And with Dad.

Her throat tightened as she realized that, once again, the most important man in her life had failed to be there when she needed him. When his daughter needed him.

How could Erin have been so blind, seeing only what she wanted to see in Jase? She'd been right. Preachers were all alike, putting everybody, even strangers, ahead of family.

And that hurt more than her father's mistakes ever had. Because she'd honestly begun to think Jase was different.

Chapter Twelve

"Jase, there's a problem."

The ER nurses were preparing Hailey for her transfer to Jackson, hanging a new IV bag and giving papers to Miss Jessie to sign, when Mama knocked on the door and opened it an inch. Her voice held the same note of anxiety he'd heard in this hospital the day he sat by Miss Fannie's bed and his mother brought the bad news of Courtney's death.

Jase shot to his feet and out to the hall. Mama's face was nearly as white as her lab jacket. The look in her eyes shot cold fear through him. "Is it Bella?"

"I don't know," she said, her voice little more than a whisper. "Marsha just called from dispatch and told me to call Pastor David. She couldn't say more because of confidentiality. I called him, and he said Rita and her boyfriend came to Rosewood to take the baby."

Take her? His heart slammed against his chest as if unable to keep up with the anger boiling inside. "Where is she? Rosewood?"

"Jase. Calm down. All I know is Erin and Bella are at the church, and the police are there."

He took off for the entrance at a dead run. *Lord, keep Bella safe—and Erin...*

Three minutes later by his car clock, he screeched to a stop beside two police cars in front of the church and jumped out as local cops questioned Rita and her big, bald boyfriend. "Eddie, where's the baby?" He ran over to the officer who'd been his classmate.

"In the church somewhere. Pastor David says she's okay." The officer opened the cruiser door and motioned the guy inside.

Pastor David met Jase at the door and unlocked it for him.

"Where's Bella? And Erin?" He glanced around the empty lobby.

"She took the baby into the sanctuary. They're still there." His pastor laid his hand on Jase's shoulder, but for once, the familiar gesture held no comfort. "They're okay. You need to calm down. If you go barreling in there, you'll scare Bella."

Right. He stood for a moment, hands on hips, blew out a couple big breaths and pretended it helped. He turned toward the sanctuary doors.

"Jase? Erin did a great job of keeping everybody safe," Pastor David said, standing guard at the entrance. "The baby, Miss Fannie and our congregation. She's amazing."

Thank You, Lord. "She proves it every day."

Jase pushed through the swinging doors to the sanctuary. Yes, Erin was not only amazing, but sweet, gentle—cute. The kind of amazing he wanted in his life and home for the rest of their lives. As soon as he found her, he'd tell her so. Ask her to stay. To be Bella's mama until enough time had passed that he could ask her to marry him.

He had to find her first.

"Erin?" The room not only sounded empty, but it felt empty, too. "It's Jase."

Nothing.

She must have taken Bella and hidden somewhere. Jase checked between the chairs, behind the pulpit and the piano. Then he glanced at the exit. She wouldn't have gone outside with Rita out there, would she?

Then his gaze fell on the door to the hallway between the sanctuary and the pastor's office. She'd no doubt seen him, Bella and Pastor David come out of there on their first Sunday.

It would be a great place to hide. He sprinted toward it. "Erin!"

He opened the door. She'd turned on the light and huddled down on the floor halfway up the hall. Now she leaned against the outer wall, cradling Bella and singing "What a Friend We Have in Jesus," her voice breaking and raw.

He'd never heard a more beautiful sound. "Erin…"

She looked up, her cheeks wet with tears and her eyes red and swollen.

"Are you okay? Is Bella all right?" He hurried to her, intending to take both her and the baby in his arms, but she got up before he had the chance.

"We're fine," she said, wiping her face with her sleeve and drawing a deep, halting breath. "I heard police cars. Did they get Rita and that guy?"

"We're all safe. They took them both in for questioning."

"I'm glad." She handed Bella over to him, kissed the top of her head. "Goodbye, sweet Bella. I love you so much."

"Wait, where are you going?"

"I honestly don't know," she said and left him standing in the empty hallway.

It took Jase a moment to figure out what had just happened. Erin had somehow rescued his child from Rita and her gorilla, had hidden Bella in the safest place available, then kissed her and walked out.

But out of what? The hallway? The church? Their lives?

He strode down the hall to the pastor's office, wishing he could sprint but afraid to while holding Bella.

In the office, Pastor David and the deacons had assembled, all talking at once and causing enough chaos that Jase might make it outside before they noticed him. At the office's glass door, he saw a dozen or more church members milling around, probably talking about the evening's events.

He sneaked out into the foyer and managed to take a whole two steps before Zeke stopped him. "What happened? How did Erin—?"

"I don't know. I need to find her."

Jase pushed through the crowd, listening to their questions and promising answers as soon as he knew anything. When he'd made his way to the door, a *Natchez Democrat* reporter blocked his way, asking the same questions as everyone else.

"I don't have any answers," he said. "I'm trying to find out." About more than just Rita.

When he made it outside, he found Bella's

car seat next to the church door. The police cars and Miss Fannie's SUV were gone.

What was going on here?

He was pretty sure no one had stolen the car, because what thief would take the time to remove a baby's seat? Erin must have driven off in the car and left the seat so he could get Bella home safely. But why would she leave alone, without telling him?

It was time to find out.

Rather than brave the crowd inside the church again, Jase pulled out his phone, called Pastor David and asked him to get someone to bring Miss Fannie outside. By the time he had the seat in the car and Bella strapped in it, Miss Fannie came out, holding Chance's arm.

"Dude, you should have seen Erin," Chance said, his eyes revealing a thirteen-year-old's crush. "She drove that SUV in here like it was your Mustang, squealed the brakes and had Bella out of the car and in the church in about three point five seconds!"

An exaggeration, Jase was sure, but still mighty impressive.

"She knew just what to do. She made Zeke lock down the church and keep everybody in the basement. I took Miss Fannie downstairs where she'd be safe, in case shooting started."

"Chance, I don't think anybody would have started shooting—"

"And she hid, and Bella was crying, and she somehow got her to be quiet. She saved Bella's life. She's a ninja!"

Well, there was probably no harm in letting him put Erin on a pedestal like that. She was certainly a hero—or a heroine—in Jase's eyes tonight. Or would be, if he knew where she was.

"Miss Fannie, we'd better head home," Jase said. "I'm pretty sure Erin took your car and is waiting for us."

As they drove the mile and a half to Rosewood, Miss Fannie gave Jase the details of the evening's events. The longer she talked, the more Jase realized Chance was right. Erin was a ninja. At least when it came to keeping a newborn baby safe.

When they got home, the house was dark and the SUV sat in the drive. Jase unfastened the car seat and carried Bella inside, Miss Fannie on his other arm.

"Erin?" Jase called, snapping on the lights. "We're home."

No answer.

"Maybe she's lying down, after all that happened," Miss Fannie said. "I'll knock on her door."

He took Bella out of her car seat and held her a moment, her soft breath warm on his hand. It seemed impossible that Rita would want Bella so much, she'd have her boyfriend threaten to come in and take her. While the law might not consider this an actual abduction attempt, it ran pretty close to the line.

"You might never know what happened to you tonight, but Erin kept you safe when I couldn't," he whispered to Bella. "I'm going to try to get her to be your mama, baby girl."

He laid her in her cradle.

"Jase, all Erin's things are gone," Miss Fannie said, coming out of Erin's room, tears streaming down her rose-petal cheeks. She handed him an envelope with his name on it. "She left us."

Taking the envelope, he somehow knew it wasn't good news. He sprinted up the stairs to his new, second-floor bedroom, where he could read the note in private.

There Jase sat at his desk and ripped open the note, the envelope shaking in his hands. He drew out a single sheet of flower-scented stationery.

Jase,
Thank you for the wonderful experience at Rosewood. Miss Fannie is healthy and

well, and you're doing a great job with Bella, so you don't need my services any longer.

Rosewood is the home I've always dreamed of. I'll never forget Windsor.

Give my love to Bella and Miss Fannie.

With appreciation,

Erin Tucker

That quickly, she was gone. He let the note slip to the floor.

The minute the ride share dropped off Erin and Tasha at Bluff Haven Bed-and-Breakfast, she knew she'd made the right choice. In accommodations, if nothing else. She settled into her room with its river view, her arms aching with emptiness, as if little Bella still belonged in them.

She had a feeling losing Bella would be one of the biggest regrets of her life. But what could she have done differently?

Erin settled into her room, unsure how long she'd stay or where she'd go when she left.

While the pull to Osaka was still strong, Rosewood had changed her. She now realized Japan wouldn't give her the satisfaction she'd had while taking care of Bella and Miss Fannie. It hardly seemed worth crossing the world in order to get there. And yet, it was the opportunity of a lifetime.

Maybe she should call Danielle. If she did, and Dannie said her boss's coworker had already found a nurse, Erin might feel better about not going. Or not.

Her meager belongings stashed away in an antique dresser, Erin stepped outside to sit on her balcony and watch the river, leaving her phone inside to resist the temptation to call Danielle. She snuggled into the wicker love seat with a heavy throw blanket and pulled Tasha up onto her lap. Her sweet little dog seemed confused, trembling in Erin's arms. "I haven't figured everything out yet either, puppy."

As Tasha settled, Erin gazed down the river to the gentle bend in the distance. At first she was disappointed that she couldn't see the little red-roofed gazebo. But after a few minutes, she was glad it was out of sight.

Because it was time to give up Jase Armstrong.

Chapter Thirteen

For the third time, a woman Jase loved had run away. And this time was the last.

After a sketchy breakfast the next morning, he carried Bella's bottle and a burp cloth into the hall, where Miss Fannie tried to comfort her. When Jase had laid the cloth on Miss Fannie's shoulder, she took the bottle from him. "I hope this makes her feel better. I've never seen her so fussy," he said.

"She probably knows Erin is gone. The house feels empty without her, and Bella senses it."

It was true. Even though they had Bella now, Rosewood felt less like a home than it had before Erin and the baby moved in.

"She won't take her bottle," Miss Fannie said. "All she wants to do is cry."

Yeah, Jase knew the feeling. He took Bella

from Miss Fannie and began walking the length of the hall and back, hoping to settle her.

A key rattled in the back door lock, and Miss Eugenia came in, carrying a basket. "I made too many biscuits this morning. So I stirred up some chocolate gravy to go with them. Have you eaten?"

"I didn't feel much like cooking this morning, so we had leftover quiche and bananas," Jase said. Surely Miss Eugenia wouldn't expect him to eat.

She marched right over to him and took her Pyrex dish of gravy out of an insulated container. Lifting the lid, she stuck the dish under his nose.

He had to admit, it smelled good…

"You know biscuits and chocolate gravy are my favorite," Miss Fannie said.

Jase gave Bella to Miss Fannie and went to the kitchen for plates and forks.

While he was there, he glanced at his phone. Erin still hadn't returned his calls or answered his texts. He'd stopped checking his phone in front of Miss Fannie at about midnight last night, since she always looked so disappointed when he had to tell her Erin hadn't replied.

"Y'all look glum this morning," Miss Eugenia said as Jase set the round table for their second breakfast.

"Erin's gone. We think she went to Japan," Miss Fannie said as Bella finally took the bottle.

"Japan?" Miss Eugenia set her biscuits on the platter Jase had brought for them from the kitchen. "That's nonsense. She's staying at Norb and Lucy Murray's inn on the bluff."

Erin—still in Natchez? "How did you find out?"

"You know the new guy who works in Rosemary's coffee shop next to the gym? He moonlights as a ride share driver, and he took Erin there last night."

"You've been to Creative Juices and Coffees already this morning?" Miss Fannie said.

Miss Eugenia pulled a bottle of blueberry kefir from her basket. "I wanted to get this to serve with our breakfast."

Only Miss Eugenia would serve health food with chocolate.

"Why did Erin move out of Rosewood?" she asked after Jase gave thanks for the food. "Just because of what happened with Bella?"

Maybe Miss Eugenia was right. He needed some biscuits and gravy this morning. He opened two biscuits on his plate, then grabbed a third and covered them with gravy as if he could hide his embarrassment as well as he could hide three big biscuits. "I...think it has something to do with me. But I wanted her to stay."

"You just wanted her to stay, or you're in love with her?" Miss Eugenia asked.

Leave it to her to put everything right out there. "Both. I think I loved Erin from the moment I panicked in the hospital parking lot, when it was time to pick up Bella. She calms me, she helps me make sense. She's smart, beautiful, sweet." He paused. "She completes me."

Miss Eugenia nodded, a faraway look in her eyes. "I felt the same way when I fell in love."

"I thought this time, I'd found someone who shared my love for the ministry. I even thought she had a calling." He took a bite of the comforting food. Miss Eugenia had been right—her perfect, flaky biscuits and creamy gravy were just what he'd needed. "It seemed right to me. Apparently, I was wrong. Without knowing what I was doing, I set myself up once again—falling for a girl who wasn't called and didn't want to be in the ministry."

"Did she say so?" Miss Eugenia had made plates for herself and Miss Fannie and now took a bite of her biscuit.

"At first, yes. You remember Calum King? The football player? His fiancée broke up with him the same week Kayla dumped me."

Miss Fannie had finished feeding and burping Bella, so she laid the infant in the cradle. "His fiancée called off the wedding because he'd missed her college graduation, right?"

"Her nurse's pinning," Miss Eugenia said.

Jase should have been surprised the ladies remembered the details. But he'd been close to them long enough to expect just about anything. He laid down his fork. "Erin was his fiancée."

"That was our Erin?" Miss Fannie stopped with her fork halfway to her mouth.

"Of course it was, Fannie. Don't you remember the picture of her with the three-legged corgi? I knew who she was the first time I saw Tasha."

As usual, Miss Eugenia was about three steps ahead of Jase. "She broke it off because Calum and her preacher father skipped her pinning to go to the hospital to pray with somebody. That's why Erin doesn't want to marry a minister. She doesn't want that kind of life."

"Have you talked to her?" Miss Eugenia filled a plate and set it in front of Miss Fannie. Then she served herself a plate as well and sat next to Jase.

"She doesn't take my calls."

"Could her actions have anything to do with

the fact that you did the same thing last night? On a smaller scale, but it's the same thing."

"But I didn't, Miss Eugenia. I prayed about it first and then checked with the kids. They wanted me to go."

"That's different. School is still out today, isn't it?" Miss Eugenia said.

"Yeah, they still don't have that water leak fixed."

She tightened her lips. "I have things to do," she said as she headed for the door.

As abrupt as her departure was, she might as well go and attend to her errands, because there was nothing she could do to bring Erin back to him. Even if she did turn out to be the famed Natchez matchmaker.

Erin had just picked up her phone, having decided to call Danielle and ask if the Osaka job had been filled, when a knock came at her door. Tasha let out her "someone's here" bark and headed back inside. Erin set the phone on the balcony table.

What would she do if it was Jase?

Another knock sounded before she could decide. "Erin, it's Eugenia Price Stratton. Please open the door."

Apparently, the shrewd lady had heard that Erin had moved out of Rosewood, and she'd probably guessed why. She likely suspected Erin wouldn't answer if she thought it was Jase.

Erin didn't know if she would have or not. She opened the door to Miss Eugenia, Darnell, Chance and Kiara.

"I brought these young people here in my golf cart because they have something to say to you."

"Please come in." Erin stood back to let them in, unable to hold back a smile, even in her misery. "Miss Eugenia, how did you know I was here?"

"Natchez is a small town" was all she said.

Apparently, not much went on in Natchez that Miss Eugenia didn't know about.

Kiara gave Erin a hug while the boys petted Tasha.

Erin hugged Kiara back, realizing how much she'd miss these kids. Then she patted Darnell's shoulder and ruffled Chance's hair. "I'm so happy you came by. What are you doing here?"

She led the way to the balcony, where they each took a seat.

"We didn't come here to say goodbye." Kiara ignored the view of the river, focusing instead on Erin. "Miss Eugenia thinks you're leaving because you believe Pastor Jase missed our play to go and help somebody else. If that's true, we want you to know you've got it all wrong."

"Hailey, Miss Jessie's granddaughter, used to be in our youth group," Darnell said. "She was being life-flighted out of our hospital, and Pastor Jase asked us what we wanted him to do—stay and watch our play or go to the hospital. We told him to go."

Oh…that changed everything.

Erin stood and went to the railing, gazed out over the river. What if Dad and Calum had asked her what she wanted them to do the night of her pinning? What would she have said?

She might have told them to go. Or she might have asked the nursing department chair to pin her first so they could leave immediately afterward.

At the bottom of all her heartache over the long-ago incident, perhaps she'd merely wanted to be important enough to them that they would ask.

She gazed at the fresh young faces of the kids she'd learned to love, almost as much as she loved Bella. How could she bear to leave them?

The biggest question was whether she could leave Jase. If she'd truly wanted to be done with him, would she have stayed here instead of boarding a plane? Did she want him to come after her, ask her to stay?

She searched her heart and found the answer to both questions was no. She wanted only to go back to him. To their home. To Rosewood.

"We don't want you to leave, Miss Erin," Darnell said. "Pastor Jase has it bad for you, and we want you to stay and get married and help him. To be one of our youth leaders."

Well, that was a bit presumptuous, but the thought was sweet.

"Love is important," Chance added. "I loved Misty for the one week we had her. If I could do something to bring her back, I would. No matter what it cost." His voice cracked a little, breaking her heart. "Don't waste a chance to love someone."

Don't waste a chance to love...

But that was what she was doing, and more. At once, she understood that, if Jase cared for her as Darnell thought, then she'd made history repeat itself for him. Because she'd just become the third woman to reject him because he was a pastor.

She had some rebuilding to do—some repentance. Some apologies to give.

But for now, she had a call to make. After she said goodbye to her guests, she reached for her phone, pulled up her contacts, found "Dad" and dialed.

Her father answered on the first ring, surprise in his voice. "Erin?"

Even through the phone, she could sense his love. His hope. She should have done this years ago.

"Dad? I just called to say I love you, and I've been wrong about a lot of things…"

Chapter Fourteen

Now that Erin had made peace with her dad, she could only hope Jase would be as forgiving.

She packed her suitcases and leashed Tasha, then waited for Miss Eugenia to come back and take her to Rosewood. If Erin had thought Darnell was presumptuous for saying she should marry Jase, then Erin was doubly presumptuous for thinking he'd want her to move back to Rosewood. If he didn't love her, she'd find a place to go, maybe home to New York. But if Darnell was right and Jase "had it bad" for her, then she'd either live at the inn until she could find a house and a job, or she'd get her luggage and settle into one of the cottages on Miss Fannie's estate.

But not like before. This time, if Jase felt the same, they'd prepare for life's biggest adventure: loving each other, loving the Lord and loving the ministry He'd given them.

Osaka could never compare to this. Besides, they could always visit there together. It would be nice not to go sightseeing alone…

A half hour later, Miss Eugenia stopped her golf cart at Rosewood's front door and went in to visit with Miss Fannie.

Erin took off Tasha's leash to let her run free on Rosewood's massive lawns. Then, since Jase would probably be in the kitchen this time of day, she took her time ambling around toward the back door, the corgi close by.

As soon as she rounded the corner of the house, she spotted Jase with his back to her, crouched down in the herb garden with his basket and shears. Which explained why Miss Eugenia had gone in the front. Miss Fannie must have told her Jase would be out here, and the ladies wanted them to be alone.

Tasha ran toward him the moment she saw him.

Erin resisted the urge to do the same.

"Tasha?" He stood, looked around, caught her gaze. The pain in his so-blue eyes nearly made her weep.

"Jase, I was wrong." She moved closer, stepped into the garden. "I'm sorry."

He sprang to his feet and covered the distance between them in seconds, his shears still in his hand. "Erin…"

"Can we talk?"

He set the shears in the grass, just outside the garden, and walked with her across the spring-green lawn to the garden cottage. "I was hoping you'd come back. I missed you, and we can hardly console Bella at times. What happened?"

"It was foolish of me," she said as they reached the cottage. "I took Bella and Miss Fannie to the church because I knew you would be there, but you weren't. When I found out you left the kids to do hospital visitation, it felt like my pinning ceremony all over again."

Jase sat beside her on the porch. "I'm sorry for that. I remembered what you'd been through, and I didn't want to hurt the teens by taking off on their special night."

"I know. Miss Eugenia brought Darnell, Chance and Kiara to the inn where I'm staying, and they told me, and I realized how I'd hurt you…"

He moved closer and brushed his fingers over her cheek, wiping away a few tears she hadn't realized she'd shed. "Erin. It's okay."

The way he said her name, his drawl deep and emotion-filled—she knew he'd forgiven her, missed her. Still wanted her in his life.

"I want to make it right." Erin caught his hand, held it tight. "I'm sorry for thinking you'd abandon the kids. I even thought that, if you'd been at the church, you could have helped me keep Bella safe. And I want you to know that, even if you don't care for me the same way…" She hesitated, a part of her still fearing the worst. "I love you, Jase."

She watched as a change took place in his eyes, joy displacing pain, a fine mistiness settling in. "Erin, I've been in love with you since the day you came to Rosewood. But we can't move forward until we settle the big issue. I'll always be a pastor."

"Yes. I realized today that a call to ministry is a call to love, to adventure—to grace. And I'm ready to accept the call."

Jase brushed back a wisp of her hair, then cupped her cheek. "You know that's a lifelong calling, not just a job, right? Once you say yes, there's no turning back."

"I don't want to turn back. I know ministry isn't glamorous. There'll be no Paris, no White House visits. It's mostly hard work and sacrifice, with lots of tears mixed in. Because we have no guarantees."

"Except this one— 'My grace is sufficient for thee: for My strength is made perfect in weakness.'" Jase stood and, before she knew what was happening, he picked up Tasha and carried her toward the house. "Meet me at the garage. I want to show you something."

Erin strolled toward the garage, taking in the beauty that was Rosewood and giving thanks to the Lord for forgiveness and healing. By the time she reached the garage, Jase came out again, a key in his hand, and they got in the car.

"Where are we going?" she asked as they turned onto Quitman Boulevard.

"To a place I've neglected since you and the baby came to Natchez. A place where we'll spend lots of time together for years to come. Maybe the rest of our lives." He flashed a grin. "I've been missing this place. I think you'll love it."

Minutes later, they pulled into a drive leading to a cute little frame home with fresh white paint and what looked like a new roof. And a perfect view of the river.

This was the last thing she'd expected. Jase, owning a home. "Do you want to move away from Rosewood?"

He came around the car to open her door. "This is River House. My mom raised Abe and me here after our dad left. I've been fixing it up for the past year. It's almost ready."

River House. "This is your youth outreach building."

"Not just a building. It's going to be a second home for the teens of Natchez, whether or not they go to my church—or any church. I want it to be a safe place for them to eat great food, get support and experience the love of Jesus."

They started up the new brick sidewalk. Jase pulled a key from his pocket and unlocked the door, held it open for her.

On the outside, River House looked like any other home on the street, although in much better condition. On the inside, it seemed designed for youth ministry, divided into a kitchen, huge living area and bathrooms. Other than the stickers still on the new windows and the refrigerator in the middle of the room, not yet hooked up, it looked nearly ready for use.

"This will soon be my home away from home," he said. "I hope it will be yours, too."

She spun around, taking in every detail. "It's the perfect second home for us."

"In that case…" He reached into his pocket, pulled out a small box and handed it to her. "I bought this for you for Valentine's Day."

Oh, how sweet. She opened the box and lifted out a silver heart necklace, then fastened it around her neck. "It's just right. I love it."

"It's too soon to propose, but I will before long. For now, will you be my girl—and Bella's mama?"

She wrapped her arms around his waist, reached up and kissed him. And he kissed her back slowly, with no trace of urgency, just a sweet assurance of a future filled with love and hope. "Yes, I will," she said, pulling away. "I'll be your girl and Bella's mama and your partner in ministry. For the rest of my life."

When the sun had set on the river, they picked up Erin's luggage at the inn and headed back to Rosewood. Miss Eugenia's golf cart was gone, and a light burned in the hall.

When they walked in the back door, Jase called out, "Miss Fannie! Our girl has come home."

Epilogue

~❧

On Valentine's Day of the following year, Jase and Erin each held one of Bella's hands as she walked between them, approaching Judge Vincent Davis's bench for their final adoption hearing.

Jase had thought this day might never come. But here it was, and he and Erin would become Bella's legal parents this morning and husband and wife in the afternoon.

And they would somehow have to get this mob of friends and family from the courtroom to Wisteria Chapel in time to finish preparing for the wedding.

After they were sworn in, Judge Davis signed the final adoption decree, and the whole gang stepped up for pictures with Bella and the judge. Then they descended on Rosewood.

The sunny, sixty-five-degree Natchez afternoon seemed just right for the simple wedding they'd planned. Friends and family enjoyed Creole charcuterie and cheese boards and drank Rosewood lemonade in the courtyard and under the wisteria-covered pergola, both decorated with twinkle lights and pink camellias.

In the midst of the music, food and visiting, Mama played with Bella and Georgia. Erin stood off to one side with her parents, continuing to reconnect with them as she had the past year, looking beautiful in her simple white dress with pink rosebuds. Zeke sat with Danielle at a secluded table, seeming to let down his tough-guy image for the first time in the six years Jase had known him. Darnell, Chance, Kiara and the other teens kept the plates and glasses full. Judge Davis visited with attorney Joseph Duncan and Rosemary's father, the recently retired Judge Williams.

"This is just like our early weddings, Jase," Miss Fannie said, joining him at the edge of the courtyard. "Simple and casual, eating food you and Erin and the boys made in our own kitchen and decorated with flowers from our gardens. It's the perfect wedding."

Yes, it was. He looked out over the crowd—Abe and Rosemary with Georgia and their baby boy, Hollis, Miss Jessie, Sister Myra from church, and a hundred other friends. A sweet sense of joy and long-abiding love and friendship permeated the air like lilac perfume and entwined each loved one with the others.

A great way to begin a new life.

Finally, Pastor David came over and squeezed Jase's shoulder. "Ready to start?"

"I'm beyond ready. Let's go."

While his pastor moved from table to table, asking the guests to start for the chapel, Jase strode to the pergola and relayed the same message. Then he stood back and watched for a moment as the crowd dispersed toward the rows of white chairs in front of the chapel, relaxed and taking their time and visiting along the way.

A perfect wedding. No stress, no schedule, no hurry, no nerves. Just a bunch of people who knew and loved each other, coming together to witness and celebrate his and Erin's love.

He met Erin at the tail end of the crowd and walked with her and Bella, alongside Miss Eugenia, who carried Miss Fannie in her golf cart.

When everybody had found the seat they wanted, Jase took his place with Abe and Pastor David.

Erin handed Bella off to her mother, who took the little girl to the front row and sat her on her lap. Then Erin's dad offered his arm, walked her to the altar and left her next to Danielle, her bridesmaid.

Pastor David opened his Bible and recited from memory, "Dearly beloved, we are gathered here today in the sight of God…"

Jase let his gaze drift across Erin's face, her beautiful brown eyes and dimpled smile, biding his time until Pastor David spoke the words he wanted to hear.

"Do you take this woman to be your wife, to live together in holy matrimony, to love her, to honor her, to comfort her and to keep her, in sickness and in health, forsaking all others for as long as you both shall live? If so, please respond by saying 'I do.'"

And just like that, the Natchez Wedding Preacher, who couldn't keep a bride, finally had the love of his life at the altar and spoke the words he'd wanted to say for so long.

"I do."

* * * * *

*If you enjoyed this story, don't miss
Christina Miller's next sweet romance,
available later this year from Love Inspired!*

*Find more great reads at
www.LoveInspired.com.*

Dear Reader,

Thank you for returning with me to my beloved Natchez, the most beautiful town on the Mississippi River! This story took me back to the days when I worked as an RN and helped my fiancé (later, my husband) in youth ministry. I've always been glad God called me to be a pastor's wife.

When Jase and Erin thought they'd never find love, they learned that all things are possible when we believe. If you have an impossible situation, I hope you'll trust Jesus to help you believe His words and find the peace that comes when He intervenes.

I'd love to hear from you! Drop me a line at Facebook.com/christinalinstrotmiller or on Twitter, @CLMillerbooks, and let me know how you're seeing the Lord do the impossible.

Christina Miller